Royce Stared At The Woman Asleep In His Bed.

In the cold, clear light of midmorning, the smoky haze of last night's passion took on a different and unsettling hue. He had slept better, deeper, than he had in nearly a year. But what was that sleep going to cost him?

Megan looked so vulnerable, so defenseless, so appealing in slumber, it took all of his control to keep from going to her, joining her on the bed, losing himself in the joy of loving her.

Loving her?

Dear Reader,

This month's lineup is so exciting, I don't know where to start...so I guess I'll just "take it from the top" with our October *MAN OF THE MONTH*. *Temptation Texas Style!* by Annette Broadrick is a long-awaited addition to her SONS OF TEXAS series. I know you won't want to miss this continuation of the saga of the Calloway family.

Next, many of you eagerly anticipated the next installment of Joan Hohl's BIG BAD WOLFE series—and you don't have to wait any longer. *Wolfe Wanting* is here!

Don't worry if you're starting these series midstream; each book stands alone as a sensuous, compelling romance. So take the plunge.

But there's much more. Four fabulous books you won't want to miss. Kelly Jamison's *The Daddy Factor;* Raye Morgan's *Babies on the Doorstep;* Anne Marie Winston's *Find Her, Keep Her;* and Susan Crosby's *The Mating Game.*

Don't you dare pick and choose! Read them all. If you don't, you'll be missing something wonderful.

All the best,

Lucia Macro
Senior Editor

Please address questions and book requests to:
Silhouette Reader Service
U.S.: 3010 Walden Ave., P.O. Box 1325, Buffalo, NY 14269
Canadian: P.O. Box 609, Fort Erie, Ont. L2A 5X3

JOAN HOHL
WOLFE WANTING

SILHOUETTE *Desire*®
Published by Silhouette Books
America's Publisher of Contemporary Romance

SILHOUETTE BOOKS

ISBN 0-373-05884-5

WOLFE WANTING

Copyright © 1994 by Joan Hohl

Printed in U.S.A.

JOAN HOHL

is the author of almost three dozen books. She has received numerous awards for her work, including the Romance Writers of America Golden Medallion award. In addition to contemporary romance, this prolific author also writes historical and time travel romances. Joan lives in eastern Pennsylvania with her husband and family.

One

She was a mess.

Royce Wolfe clenched his teeth and gave another yank on the driver's-side door of the mangled sports car. A grunt of satisfaction vibrated his throat as the door popped open. The interior light flashed on. Pushing the door back, he stepped into the opening.

The woman was slumped over the steering wheel, her face concealed by a mass of long, dark red hair. A frown of annoyed disapproval tugged at his brows and lips.

She was not wearing the seat belt.

Royce shook his head and reached inside, grimacing at the faint but unmistakable scent of alcohol.

Booze and rain-slick roads were a deadly combination.

Brushing the long tresses aside, he pressed his fingertips to her throat. The pulse was rapid, but strong.

The deflated air bag, now draped limply over the wheel, had very likely saved her life.

The woman moaned, and her eyelashes fluttered.

"It's all right," Royce said, giving her shoulder a comforting pat. "Help's on the way," he assured her, catching the sound of sirens in the distance, swiftly approaching from opposite directions.

"Wha-what hap—?" The woman blinked, then squeezed her eyes shut, in obvious pain.

"You went off the road," Royce said, answering her unfinished question. "Crashed into the guardrail."

And you were going like hell. Royce kept the disgusted observation to himself. The information would go into his report, but right now, she had enough to contend with.

A drop of water fell from the wide brim of his hat and splashed onto her pale cheek. The woman flinched. Royce pulled back, away from the opening. Cold rain pattered on his hat and slicker.

March. Where was spring?

Royce shivered, and shifted his bleak gaze, first back the way he had come, then toward town. The wail of the sirens was louder, closer, as the vehicles converged, lights flashing atop the ambulance and police car.

Well, at least it isn't snow, he thought, shooting a glance at the woman as the vehicles came to a screeching stop—the ambulance facing him, opposite the sports car, the other vehicle, Pennsylvania State Police emblazoned on its side, directly behind his own car.

"She's alive," Royce said to the paramedic who jumped from the driver's side.

"What you got here, Sergeant?" the police officer asked, loping up to Royce.

"Hi, Evans," Royce said, acknowledging him. "Female, all alone," he said, sending a spray of rainwater flying with a jerk of his head toward the car. "Shot out of Pine Tree Drive, back there." Water ran in a narrow stream from the brim of his hat as he inclined his head to indicate the side road, less than a quarter of a mile back. "Cut right in front of me, doing at least seventy. She lost it almost at once. I had no sooner taken off after her in pursuit when she plowed into the rail."

"Drinking?" Evans asked, stepping closer to the sports car to give it the once-over.

"I caught a whiff of alcohol." Royce shrugged. "But I don't know if it was above the legal level." He raised his voice to the two paramedics working to ease the woman from the car. "You guys come across a purse?"

"Yeah," the man who had entered the vehicle from the passenger side replied. "Just found it." He handed it to the man outside, who passed it to Royce.

"Thanks," he muttered. "Can you tell if she's going to be all right?"

"Can't see anything major from here," the paramedic said. "Won't know for sure until we get her out of here and back to the hospital."

"Need the jaws?" Royce asked, referring to the jawlike apparatus used to pry mangled metal apart, commonly called the Jaws of Life.

"Naw," he said. "She's regaining consciousness, and if she can move to help, there's enough room for her to slide out from between the wheel and the seat." The man ran a quick glance over the front of the car. "But I'm certain you're gonna need a wrecker for this heap."

"Yeah." Royce shared the man's opinion.

"I'll call for one, and get some flares set up," Evans offered, turning away. He took two steps, then turned back, a frown drawing his brows together. "Didn't you go off duty at eleven, Sergeant?"

"Supposed to," Royce answered. "I stayed to finish some paperwork, left the barracks around eleven-thirty. I was on my way home when this lady cut out of the road in front of me." While he was speaking, he kept an eye on the paramedics, monitoring their progress as they transferred the woman from the car to a gurney, then to the rear of the ambulance.

"How's she doing?" he asked.

"Okay," one of the men answered. "She managed to slide out, but she's lost consciousness again."

A gust of wind blew rain under the wide brim of his hat and into his face. Royce shivered.

"Why don't you go on home now?" Evans suggested. "I'll ask for assistance when I call for a wrecker, then I'll go on in to the hospital."

The rear ambulance door thunked shut. Royce started for his car, shaking his head. "Night like this, we need every man on the roads." He opened the door, shucked out of his slicker, then slid behind the wheel. It felt good to get out of the stiff coat and the pouring rain. "You wait here for the wrecker," he said, tossing the woman's purse and his hat onto the passenger's seat. "I'll follow the ambulance into town. I live only a couple of blocks away from the hospital. I'll go home after I've talked to the woman, and I'll file a report in the morning."

"Whatever you say, Sergeant." Evans sketched a salute of thanks for being spared the chore of the extra paperwork, then strode to his car.

Royce tailed the ambulance into the small town of Conifer, Pennsylvania, and pulled alongside the covered, brightly lit entrance to Conifer General Hospital's emergency unit, where the ambulance had parked.

Having been alerted to expect an accident victim, a nurse and two orderlies were awaiting their arrival. Since Royce's assistance was obviously not required, he took a few minutes to fish the woman's wallet from her purse before stepping out of the car. Flipping it open, he read the information on her driver's license.

The first thing that caught his eye was her picture. It was not great, yet even with the inferior quality of the photograph, she was clearly not unattractive. Then his eyes shifted to her name.

Megan Delaney. Nice name, Royce thought absently, his eyes moving up the laminated card, past the issue date, to the medical restrictions. Must wear corrective lenses. Hmm... There had been no sign of glasses when he brushed her hair away from her face. Had they flown off on impact, or was she wearing contact lenses? Check it out.

His eyes moved again, skimming over the expiration date, classes, endorsements and driver ID number, and came to rest on birth date.

The woman was twenty-seven years and three months old—eight years his junior.

Old enough to know better than to drink and drive, Royce thought, especially on a rain-slick road.

His eyes skipped over the top line of information, and settled on one tiny section. Blue eyes. Big surprise, for a redhead he reflected, closing the wallet.

Royce glanced up at the sound of the automatic entrance doors swishing open. With the nurse leading the way, the orderlies were pushing the gurney into the building. Gripping the purse, he stepped out of the car, gave a casual wave to the paramedics and followed the group inside.

"Hey, Sarge!" a fresh-faced young nurse called out cheekily from behind the desk just inside the doors.

"Don't tell me you've given up the desk job to go back on road duty again!"

"Okay, I won't tell you that," Royce drawled, flashing a teasing grin at her. "You want to hit the release?" he said, inclining his head toward the second set of automatic doors, which for safety reasons were activated by buttons accessible only to hospital personnel.

"Sure."

The doors parted, and with a murmured thank-you, Royce stepped through the opening.

"*Are* you back on highway duty?" the nurse called after him.

Royce paused in the opening, keeping the doors apart. "No," he answered. "I was on my way home when this woman crashed into the guardrail. And, since I was coming into town anyway..." He shrugged.

"Gotcha." The nurse turned her attention to a man who came limping up to the desk, but slyly observed, "By the way, Sarge, I must tell you that your red handbag definitely clashes with your uniform."

Responding to her teasing comment with a dry look, Royce continued past the doors, which closed behind him, and to the doorway of a long room containing a row of curtained cubicles. The orderlies were pushing the now-empty gurney from the last cubicle.

"Hi, Sarge," one of the men said as Royce passed by on his way to the cubicle. "Haven't seen you in here for a while. Where have you been hiding out?"

"Behind a desk," Royce answered. "Where it's dry and warm. No mangled bodies. No blood. No gore."

"Nice work if you can get it," the other man said, grinning. As he pushed the gurney through the doorway, he called over his shoulder, "I just love your purse."

"Yeah." Royce didn't return the grin or respond to the good-natured gibe as he normally would have. This little jaunt to the hospital stirred too many unpleasant memories, strongly reminding him of his reasons for having accepted the desk job when it was offered to him six months ago.

Royce was a good cop. If pressed, he would have had to admit, without exaggeration or conceit, that he was a damn good cop. But, with over ten years with the state police, investigating robberies, working on drug busts and patrolling the highways, he had had his fill of trips to the hospital with torn, bleeding and sometimes dead bodies.

The day would come when, restless and tired of pushing papers, Royce would request a transfer back to highway patrol. But until that day arrived, he'd just as soon avoid the distinctive scents of disinfectant and medicine.

Royce wrinkled his nose at the assault on his senses by the familiar smell, and shoved the curtain aside.

"Doc Louis not here, Jill?" he asked the nurse, a middle-aged woman who had been on duty in Emergency for as long as he had been on duty in the Conifer district. She was standing by the gurney where the woman lay, taking her pulse.

The nurse frowned, concentrating on the pulse count. "Busy down the line," she said, gently laying the woman's arm by her side. "He's stitching a head wound."

"Accident?"

"No." Jill gave him a tired smile, and a shrug of resignation. "Knife fight in a barroom. As you can see, we're pretty busy, and stretched mighty thin. Dr. Hawk's splinting a finger—a slightly inebriated teenager slammed a car door on it." She sighed. "Just the usual Friday-night fun and games."

"Yeah." Royce grimaced.

The nurse frowned. "What are you doing here? I thought you were riding a desk now."

"I am." Royce suppressed his growing impatience; he was getting pretty tired of answering the same question. "I just happened to be close by when the lady decided to test the strength of the guardrail." He shifted his eyes to the ashen-faced woman. "She all right?"

"Looks like all surface injuries. A few cuts, abrasions, bruises—a lot of bruises—but..." She lifted her shoulders in another shrug. "I'm sure the doctor will want X rays after a more thorough examination."

Royce nodded.

The woman on the gurney moaned.

Jill gave her a sharp-eyed look. "She's coming around. If you'll stay here with her, make sure she doesn't roll off the gurney—" she moved past him "—I'll go see if I can take over for one of the doctors."

"Will do," Royce agreed. "Don't stop for a coffee break along the way... okay?"

She grinned at him. "Not even if I bring you a cup on the house?"

"No, thanks." He grimaced. "I've tasted what that machine passes off as coffee."

"It grows on you," she said, laughing, as she pushed aside the curtain.

"That's what I'm afraid of," he drawled, smiling at her retreating back.

A low moan sounded next to Royce, wiping the smile from his face. Turning, he placed her purse at the bottom end of the gurney, then moved closer to the other end to gaze down at the fragile-looking woman.

She moaned again. Then her eyelashes fluttered and lifted, and he found himself staring into incredibly lovely, if presently clouded, sapphire blue eyes.

The license photo did her a terrible disservice, Royce realized absently. Even with the nasty bruises marring the right side of her face, Megan Delaney was not merely attractive, she was flat-out, traffic-stopping gorgeous.

Facial bruises? Royce frowned, and took a closer look. Why hadn't the air bag protected her from—

She moaned again, louder this time, scattering his thoughts, demanding his full attention.

The clouds of confusion in her eyes were dissipating, and she moved, restlessly, in obvious pain.

Following the nurse's request, Royce stepped closer, until his thigh pressed against the gurney. Bending over her, he placed his right arm on the other side of the gurney to prevent her rolling off, onto the floor.

"It's all—" he began, but that was as far as he got in his attempt to reassure her, because she screamed, drowning the sound of his voice.

"Get away from me!"

Royce started, shocked by the sheer terror evidenced by Megan Delaney's shrill voice and fear-widened eyes. Her hands flew up defensively, and she began striking at his face. One of her fingernails, broken and jagged-edged, caught his skin, scratching his cheek from the corner of his right eye to his jaw.

"What the hell?" he exclaimed, jerking backward and grabbing her wrists to keep her hands still.

She continued to scream, struggling wildly against his hold. "Get away! Don't touch me!"

"What in the world is going on in here, Sergeant Wolfe?" The voice was sharp, authoritative, and definitely female. Recognizing it, Royce sighed with relief.

"Damned if I know, Dr. Hawk," he answered, shooting a baffled look at her as she came to a stop beside him. "She took one look at me and started screeching like a banshee." He winced as Megan Delaney let out another piercing cry. "Maybe you can do something with her." Releasing Megan's wrists, he moved aside to give the doctor access to the patient.

"Get him away!" Megan sobbed, clutching at the doctor's white lab coat. "Please, get him away!"

Dr. Hawk gave him a quick glance of appeal. "If you'd wait in the corridor?"

"Sure," Royce said, relieved to comply. Turning smartly, he strode from the cubicle, then from the room.

Shaken by the experience, by the injured woman's strange reaction to his attempt to help her, Royce stood in the corridor, unmindful of the usual Friday-night bustle and activity going on around him.

"What happened to your face?"

The startled-sounding question jerked Royce into awareness. He glanced around to meet Jill's surprise-widened eyes. "That woman in there attacked me," he said, his voice revealing his sense of amazement.

"Why?" Jill looked as baffled as he felt.

"Damned if I know." Royce shook his head, trying to collect his thoughts. "She opened her eyes, took one look at me, and began carrying on like a de-mented person, screaming and hitting me. Her nails scraped my face."

"I'll say," Jill observed, leaning toward him for a closer look at his face. "It's open. Come with me and—"

Royce cut her off, dismissing the scratch with a flicking hand movement. "It's nothing."

"It's open," Jill repeated in a no-nonsense tone. "It needs cleaning and an antiseptic." She drew a breath

and leveled a hard stare at him. "Now come with me."
It was not a request; it was a direct order.

Pivoting, Jill marched down the corridor with the
erect bearing of a field marshal, obviously confident
that Royce would meekly follow.

And he did. A smile quirked his lips as he trailed in
the nurse's wake. Here he was, a sergeant in the
Pennsylvania State Police, six feet five inches of
trained law-enforcement officer, docilely obeying the
dictates of a nurse who stood no more than five feet
four inches in her rubber-soled shoes.

But she was a head nurse, Royce recalled, suppressing an impulse to chuckle. Besides, Jill had always reminded him of his mother. Not in appearance, for
there was no physical resemblance between the two
women, but in manner—kinda bossy, but gentle and
caring.

Jill led the way into a small room at the end of the
corridor, and indicated the examining table in the
center of the floor.

"Have a seat," she said, turning to a cabinet placed
close by, along one wall.

Sitting down on the very edge of the table, Royce
watched with amusement as she collected cotton
swabs, sterile packets of gauze, a plastic bottle of antiseptic and a small tube of antibiotic ointment.

"All that paraphernalia for a little scratch?" he
asked in a teasing drawl.

Jill threw him a dry look. "Do I tell you how to
conduct the business of law enforcement?"

"Point taken," he conceded, turning his head to allow her better access to his cheek.

Royce winced at the sting of whatever it was Jill swabbed on the cut to clean it.

"Big tough guy," she murmured, laughter woven inside her chiding tone.

"Don't push your luck, Jill." The warning was empty, and she knew it.

Jill laughed aloud. "What are you going to do if I push my luck?" she asked, smearing the ointment along the length of the scratch. "Throw me in the slammer?"

Royce grunted, but didn't answer; his bluff had been called. In truth, Jill's remark was straight on target. Royce had something of a reputation for being tough, simply because he *was* tough. But never, ever, did he assume the role of tough cop with women, even felons. It was not in his nature. Royce treated women, all women, with respect...even the ones who didn't deserve it.

"The ointment should do it," Jill said, breaking into his thoughts. "I think we can dispense with the bandage." She turned away to return the ointment to the cabinet.

"Thanks." Royce raised a hand to his cheek.

"Don't touch it!" Jill ordered, heaving an impatient sigh. "I just cleaned it, for goodness' sake. And now you want to put your dirty hands all over it."

Royce grinned at her. He couldn't help it. Jill was the only female he knew who said "for goodness' sake" in that particular tone of exasperation. However, he did hastily pull his hand away from his face.

"Men." Jill shook her head as she returned to stand in front of him, preventing him from rising from the table. "So, *Sergeant* Wolfe," she said, with a heavy emphasis on the title, "what did you do in there to earn yourself that scratch?" She jerked her head to indicate the other room. "Did you start grilling that poor woman before she was fully conscious or something?"

"Of course not." Royce's sharp reply let her know he resented the charge. "I tried to reassure her that everything would be fine, but the minute I started to speak, she went nuclear on me." He shook his head in bewilderment. "I mean, she went off like a bomb, screaming and striking out at my face. Hell, I didn't know what to do with her, so I caught hold of her wrists. Fortunately, that's when Doc Hawk came into the room and rescued me."

Jill frowned. "Strange."

"Strange?" Royce mirrored her reflection. "Try *weird*. This has never happened to me before." He shrugged. "After ten years on the force, I've seen enough accident victims to understand shock and trauma. But damned if I've ever seen anyone fight against someone trying to help them."

"Neither have I," Jill said sympathetically. "But she seems to have quieted down now." She smiled. "Dr. Hawk is very good at calming agitated patients."

"Yeah, I know. She's great." Royce moved restlessly.

Understanding his silent message, Jill stepped away from in front of him and headed for the door. "I think I'll go check out the situation."

"I'll go with you." Royce smiled and held up his hands placatingly when she shot him a narrow-eyed look. "Only as far as the corridor, I swear."

"Okay, let's go." She marched from the room.

Laughing to himself, Royce again trailed in her wake.

He cooled his heels for twenty-odd minutes, passing the time with the hospital personnel as they wandered by. At regular intervals, Royce sent sharp glances toward the door of the cubicled room, his impatience growing as he waited for some word from either the doctor or Jill. He was tired, and it was now past one-thirty in the morning.

Royce wanted to go home to bed. Leaning against the corridor wall, out of the way of the back-and-forth traffic, he yawned, stole another look at his watch, and contemplated storming into the room and the cubicle where the victim was confined. He was pushing away from the wall, determined to at least call Jill from the room, when the doctor came through the doorway, carrying the patient's chart and purse.

"I'm sorry to keep you waiting so long." Dr. Hawk offered him a tired smile. "But, when I explain, I'm certain you will understand the reason, Royce." Her use of his first name said much about the working friendship they had established.

"Problems, Virginia?" Royce arched his gold-tipped brows. "You sound troubled."

"She was attacked," she said, getting right to the point. "Before the crash."

"What?" Royce went rigid. "Was she—"

"No, she wasn't violated," she answered, before he had finished asking. "She managed to get away from the man. That's why her seat belt wasn't fastened." A grim smile curved her usually soft mouth. "She was thinking, rather wildly, about flight, not driver safety."

"And that's why she went wild with me."

"Yes. She opened her eyes, saw a large man looming over her, and . . ."

"Thought she was right back in the situation," Royce said, completing the explanation for her.

"Precisely."

"Bastard," he muttered.

"My sentiments exactly." Virginia Hawk expelled a deep sigh. "She is still in shock, traumatized."

Royce gave her a shrewd look. "Are you trying to tell me I can't question her?"

"You got it, Sarge," she said. "She is in no condition to be questioned. From my examination, I feel quite positive that her injuries are all external, but I'm having X rays done to confirm my opinion."

"So, if your diagnosis is confirmed, I'll talk to her afterward," he said. "I'll wait."

"No." She shook her head. "If my diagnosis is confirmed, I'm going to sedate her."

"My report, Virginia," he reminded her gently. "You know the rules."

She smiled. "I also know who is in charge here," she reminded him, just as gently. "Royce, that young woman has been through enough for one night. She needs rest, escape. Your report can wait until morning." Her tone was coaxing now. "Can't it?"

Royce was always a sucker for a soft, feminine entreaty. He gave in gracefully. "Yeah, okay."

"You've got a kind heart, Sergeant Wolfe," she said. "I told my husband so from the first day I met you." Her eyes teased him. "You're almost as nice as he is."

"Almost as tough, too," Royce drawled, recalling the tall Westerner she was married to.

Virginia Hawk laughed. "I'd say it's a toss-up." She ran a professional glance over him. "Right now, you appear ready to cave. Go home to bed, Royce. Come back in the morning. I'll prepare her for you."

"Okay." Royce looked at the woman's purse. "But first, I'd better check for next of kin, see if there's anybody—a husband, relatives—I should contact."

"I asked. She said no."

"She has no one?"

"Oh, she has family. Her parents retired, five, six months ago. They're on a cruise they planned and saved years for." Virginia sighed. "She doesn't want them notified."

"No husband, boyfriend?"

"Boyfriend?" She arched her fine blond brows.

"Okay, man friend, significant other." He shrugged. "Whatever happens to be current."

"Apparently not." Her lips curved into a taunting smile. "But it wouldn't matter if there were. She said she didn't want anyone notified. End of story, Royce."

His lips twitched. "You know what, Doc?"

"What?"

"You're even tougher than either your husband or I—and maybe even my superior officer."

Dr. Hawk laughed delightedly. "Bank on it."

"Good night, Doctor." Laughing with her, Royce turned and started for the automatic doors. Then memory stirred, and he stopped, keeping the doors open. "By the way, I think she's wearing contact lenses."

"She was." Virginia grinned. "I found them."

"Good, I'm outta here." He took a step, then paused again. "But I'll be back bright and early," he called over his shoulder. "And if anybody tries to prevent me from seeing her, you're going to see *real* tough. And you can take *that* to the bank."

Two

She was waiting for him.

Megan was sitting straight up in bed, her legs folded beneath her, her fingers picking at the lightweight white hospital blanket draped over her knees.

Dr. Hawk had said the Pennsylvania State Police sergeant would very likely be paying her a visit early this morning. That had been when the doctor was making her regular rounds, about seven-thirty or so. It was now nearing nine. Breakfast was over—the nurse's aide had been in to remove the tray from the room thirty minutes ago.

So, where was he? Megan asked herself, unconsciously gnawing on her lower lip. Where was this law officer Dr. Hawk had told her about, the one who bore the mark of Megan Delaney on his cheek?

A shudder ripped through Megan's slender body. Lord! Had she really struck . . . scratched the face of a policeman?

She must have, for not for a second could she convince herself that the doctor would have said she had, if in fact she had not.

Tears blurred Megan's vision. Absently raising a hand, she brushed the warm, salty moisture from her eyes with impatient fingers. She never cried . . . well, hardly ever.

But then, she never struck, hit or scratched people, either, Megan reminded herself. At least not until now.

But there were extenuating circumstances, Megan thought defensively. She hadn't been in her right and normal mind at the time, and she had had excellent reason for striking out at the man . . . or at least at the man she believed him to be at that particular moment.

But where was he?

Megan was not stupid. She realized that she would very likely not be too stable—emotionally, psychologically—for an extended period. Scars would remain, perhaps indefinitely.

It was not a pleasant prospect to contemplate.

On the other hand, unless she kept her mind occupied, it could slip into a reflective mode, recalling—

No! Megan slammed a mental door on that train of thought. She would need to explain the circumstances to the state cop, relive that choking terror.

Where was *he?*

Megan just wanted it all over with, the horror, humiliation and degradation of the memory. And she wanted nothing more than to crawl into a hole and hide.

She was trembling—no, shaking—with nerves and trepidation when he walked into the room fifteen minutes later.

Megan knew him immediately. She did not, of course, recognize him, as one would a friend or acquaintance. He was not in uniform. His attire was casual—jeans, a striped cotton shirt, a tweed sports coat. Fairly new, and rather expensive-looking, leather slip-ons encased his feet. Actually, he looked somewhat like a construction worker on his day off.

But Megan knew exactly who he was at first sight.

He did not stride into the room, fueled by self-importance. In truth, though, he did radiate an aura of importance and intimidation.

He was tall. Lord, was he tall! He was blond, not yellow blond, but golden blond, a shade that would likely be called sun-kissed brown, she supposed. His shoulders and chest were broad, flatly muscular; his waist and hips were narrow, his legs straight, long-boned. And he was good-looking...too good-looking. The comparison of a classic Greek statue sprang to mind; Megan dismissed it at once. No statue she had ever gazed upon in awe, up close or on film, looked that good, that attractive, nearly perfect.

All of which should not have mattered to Megan in the least at that particular point in time, but somehow did.

"Miss Delaney?"

Even his voice was golden, smooth and rich as warm amber velvet. The sound of it set Megan's teeth on edge. She swallowed, quickly, swallowed again, failed to work up enough moisture even to allow speech, then replied with a curt nod.

He was prepared, which told her a lot about him.

"Sergeant Wolfe, Pennsylvania State Police." He raised his hand, palm out, displaying his identification as he moved nearer to the bed for her to examine it up close.

Megan wanted to feel pressured, put-upon, persecuted, but she couldn't. She wanted to scream a demand to be left alone. But she couldn't do that, either. She looked at his face, at the long red scratch from his eye to his jaw, and felt sick inside—even sicker than she already felt.

"I . . . I, er . . . I'm sorry." Megan felt a hot sting behind her eyelids, and lowered her gaze. Damn! She would not cry. She would not let this man, any man, bear witness to her weakness.

"Sorry?" He frowned. "For what?"

The hot sting vanished from her eyes. Her head snapped up. Her eyes narrowed. Was this a trick? What could possibly be his purpose for playing this

"For what" game? He knew full well what she was sorry for.

"Your face," she said, unaware that her voice had lost a small corner of its frailty. "I've marked you, however unintentionally, and I'm sorry."

"Oh, that?" He moved the hand he still held aloft near to his face, and drew his index finger the length of the scratch. "It's surface. I'm not branded for life." Then he smiled, and damned if his smile wasn't golden brown, as well.

How could she think of startlingly white teeth as golden brown? Megan chided herself, staring in near-mesmerized fascination at him. And yet it was. His smile lit up not only his face, but the entire room, like a burst of pure golden sunlight through a dark and angry cloud.

Megan didn't like it. She didn't trust it. But there wasn't a thing she could do about it. She had run her car, her beautiful new car, into a guardrail. And this…this golden-haired, golden-smiled one-up-on-a-Greek-god was the law. He was in charge here. Although he hadn't yet given so much as a hint of flaunting his authority, he was in a position to do so.

Just get it over with.

The cry rang inside Megan's head, its echo creating an ache to fill the void of its passing. Suddenly, she needed to weep, she needed to sleep, she needed to be left alone. Distracted, agitated, she lifted a hand to rub her temple.

"Pain?"

Megan wasn't quite sure which startled her more, the sharp concern in his voice, or the sudden sound of his ID folder snapping shut. Before she could gather her senses enough to answer, he was moving to the door.

"I'll get a nurse."

"No!" She flung out her hand—as if she could reach him, all the way near the door, from her bed. "I'm all right. It's just a dull headache."

He turned back to run an encompassing look over her pale face, his startling blue eyes probing the depths of her equally blue, though now lackluster, eyes.

"You sure?" One toasty eyebrow climbed up and under the silky lock of hair that had fallen onto his forehead.

"Positive." Megan sighed, and nodded. "Please, have a seat." She indicated the chair placed to one side of the bed. "I'd like to get this over with."

"Well . . ." He brushed at the errant lock of hair as he slowly returned to her bedside. "If you're sure you don't need anything for pain?" The brow inched upward again.

"I'm sure," she answered, suppressing yet another sigh. "It'll pass."

"All things do."

Strangely convinced that his murmured reply was not merely the voicing of conventional comfort, but a genuine and heartfelt belief, Megan watched him lower his considerable length into the average-size chair.

He should have appeared funny, folded into the small seat, and yet he didn't. He looked . . . comfortable.

"In your own words, Miss Delaney," he said, offering her a gentle smile. "And in your own time." He glanced at his watch. "I'm in no hurry."

Megan felt inordinately grateful for his compassion and understanding. She dreaded the coming purge, the dredging up of details, the accompanying resurgence of fear.

"I . . . I . . ."

"Start at the very beginning," he inserted, his voice soft with encouragement.

"Thank you, Sergeant, I—" She broke off when he raised a hand in the familiar "halt" gesture.

"Let's make this as easy as possible. Considering the circumstances, I think we can dispense with the *sergeant* and *sir* stuff. Okay?" Both toasty brows peaked.

"Yes, but what *should* I call you?"

"My name's Royce," he said. "Royce Wolfe."

Royce Wolfe. Megan tested the name silently, deciding at once that she liked it. "Okay, Royce," she agreed, "but on one condition. And that is that you call me Megan."

"Deal." His teeth flashed in a disarming smile. Withdrawing a notebook and pen from his jacket pocket, he settled into the chair. "Whenever you're ready . . . Megan."

"I have one question."

"Shoot."

"Well, you said I should start at the beginning," she said, frowning. "Where? Of the evening, of the atta—" The very word stuck in her throat.

Megan drew a breath before trying another attempt; Royce was faster.

"You can start from the day of your birth," he suggested, quite seriously. "If that's easier for you."

"My birth?" Megan frowned again. "Why, I was born right here, in Conifer. I grew up here, lived here until I went away to college." The frown line smoothed at the realization that starting from the very beginning *was* easier.

"That was probably before I was assigned to duty here," Royce reasoned aloud. "What college did you attend?"

"Kutztown State, now University." She smiled. "It offered a great fine-arts program."

"You're an artist?" He sounded impressed.

"No." Oddly, Megan hated having to disillusion him. "It didn't take long to discover that I wasn't good enough for that. I'm an illustrator."

Royce was quick to correct her. "Illustrators are artists. Norman Rockwell was an illustrator, and so was the first of the painting Wyeths...."

"Well, yes, of course, but...". Megan broke off to frown at him. How had they strayed from the point, and what difference did it make, anyway? "Does it matter?"

"Not really." Royce grinned at her. "But you are a lot less nervous than when I came in."

Megan smiled. She couldn't help smiling. "Yes, I am. Thank you."

"You're welcome." His voice was low, honeyed, encouraging. "Ready to continue?"

"Yes. Where was I?"

"You didn't return to Conifer after college," he said, prompting her.

"Oh, right." Megan shrugged. "I had decided that to succeed, I would have to go where the action was—that being New York City, naturally."

"Naturally," he concurred in a drawl.

"I was right, you know."

"I don't doubt it." Royce appeared extremely relaxed in the small chair. "I personally wouldn't like to live there," he added. "But I don't doubt that you were right."

Megan sighed—damned if he hadn't hit the nail directly on the head.

"After all this time, I finally discovered that I personally don't like living there, either," she confessed. "That's why I jumped at the excuse to come home for a while."

"You've lost me," Royce said, in obvious confusion. "Jumped at what excuse?"

"To house-sit for my parents while they're away." She smiled, and explained, "My parents left three weeks ago on a world cruise. They'll be gone a year."

"A whole year!"

"Yes. Wild, huh?"

"It sounds great." Royce chuckled. "I wish I could talk my mother into something like that."

"Your mother's alone?" Megan asked, interested, but still conscious of playing for time, keeping the moment of truth at bay for a little longer.

"Yeah." Royce exhaled. "We lost my dad almost two years ago." He looked pensive for a moment, and then he mused aloud, "Maybe I'll talk to my brothers about all of us chipping in on a cruise vacation for Mom, if only for a week or two."

"I always wanted a brother." Megan's voice held a note of wistful yearning. "How many do you have?"

"Three," he said, laughing. "And we were a handful for my mother. Still are, at times."

"Sounds like fun." Megan sighed in soft, unconscious longing. "If I had a brother, he would..." Her voice faded, and she stared into space through eyes tight and hot, yearning for a brother, her father, someone to be there for her, hold her, protect her, tell her she was safe.

There was a moment of stillness. Then a blur of movement on the bed near her hip caught her eye. Blinking, Megan lowered her gaze and focused on the broad male hand resting, palm up, on the mattress. Without thought or consideration, she slid her palm onto his. His fingers flexed and closed around hers, swallowing her hand within the comforting protection of his.

A sense of sheer masculine strength enveloped Megan. Not a threatening, intimidating strength, but an unstated, soothing I'm-here-for-you strength, the strength she needed now, when her own had been so thoroughly, horribly decimated.

Megan blinked again, touched, and grateful for the gentle offering from this gentle giant. Unaware of her own flicker of power, she gripped his hand, hard, hanging on for sanity's sake to the solid anchor, seeking a measure of stability in her suddenly unstable world.

"It may be easier to get it over with."

Royce's soft advice echoed, joined forces with her own earlier silent demand.

"Yes." Megan's voice was little more than a breathless whisper. "I have friends who own a getaway place in the mountains," she began, steadily enough. "They called me up yesterday, said they had come in for the weekend, and invited me to meet them for dinner at the French Chalet. You know where that is?" She met his eyes; they were fixed on her face.

"Yes." Royce nodded. "In the mountains, along that side road you shot out of onto the highway in front of me."

"Did I?" Megan swallowed. "I...I never saw you."

"I know...now." His smile was faint, but encouraging. "Please, go on."

"We had a great reunion, and a lovely dinner." She paused, and then rushed on. "I had two glasses of wine, but that's all, only the two small glasses."

"Easy." His tone soothed. "I got the results of your blood-alcohol test."

Megan released the breath she'd been holding, relieved to know that at least she wouldn't be facing a drunk-driving citation in addition to yesterday's experience.

"Continue," he said gently.

"After dinner, my friends decided to stay for the music, do a little dancing. I...I was tired, and said I'd pass on the entertainment. I left...and..." Megan shut her eyes as memory swirled, filling her mind with a replayed image. "The parking lot was already filled when I'd arrived, and I had to park way in the back, at the edge of the forest," she explained in a reedy whisper. "But when I left, the lot had emptied out. My car was the only one back there."

Megan hesitated, drawing in short, panting breaths. With her inner eyes, she could see the lot, see her car, see herself hurrying to the car, unlocking it, sliding behind the wheel, inserting the key in the ignition even as she tugged on the door to pull it shut.

"I was closing the car door when...suddenly it was yanked wide open again . . . jerking my arm . . . pulling me down and sideways, nearly out of the car." Her breathing was now shallow, quick, and the words were tumbling out of her parched throat.

"Then there was a large shape looming into the opening. A hairy-backed hand grabbed my shoulder... shoved me down... and back inside." She was trembling, uncontrollably, and she was unaware of her fingernails digging into the flesh of the hand clasping hers. "My face...the side of my face scraped the steering wheel as I was pushed down...down..."

Reliving the horror, Megan didn't hear the door to her room open, didn't notice the figure of Dr. Hawk standing just inside the door, quiet, watchful, poised to go into action should she deem her patient in need of her attention.

"He was all over me!" she cried in a terrified croak. "The hand that had grabbed my shoulder moved down to clutch at my breast! His...his other hand..." She was gasping now, barely able to articulate. "He shoved that hand between my legs!"

"I'm here. You're safe."

Soft. Rock-steady. Royce's voice penetrated the ballooning fog of panic permeating Megan's mind. The fog retreated. Her entire body shaking from reactive tremors, she clung desperately to his hand and purged the poison from her system.

"Somehow I managed to work one of my legs up, between his. I...I...*rammed* my knee into his groin! He cried out, 'you bitch!' and hit me, in the face... Then he pulled back...just enough so that I could raise my leg farther. I worked my foot up to his belly. And then...and then, I pushed again, as hard as I could. He...he fell back, onto the macadam."

"Go on."

"I—I—" Megan choked, coughed, sniffed, swiped her free hand over cheeks wet from tears she was unaware of having shed. "I...don't remember, exactly.

I turned the key as I struggled up, behind the wheel. I drove away from there...from *him*...with the door wide open. I don't know when or where I thought to pull it shut. All I knew, all I could think, was that I had to get away!''

Megan heard wrenching sobs, and didn't even know they came from her tight, aching throat.

"I don't remember hitting the guardrail!" She blinked, stared, and found sanctuary in the compassion-filled blue eyes staring back at her.

"I don't re— I don't re—"

"It's over," he inserted in a low, calming voice. "It doesn't matter. Let it go."

"Yes. Yes." Megan's chin dropped onto her chest, and she began to cry, not harsh, wracking sobs, but a quiet weeping of utter exhaustion.

They let her cry, the state cop and the doctor, let her weep the catharsis of healing tears.

Megan fell asleep with her hand still gripping his.

Three

Damn, she was tall!

Megan Delaney was being released from the hospital this morning. Royce had offered to drive her home.

He felt a tingling thrill of pleasure as he stared at the woman standing next to the hospital bed—a thrill of pleasure that contained a hint of attraction. Being so tall himself, Royce did appreciate height in a woman, but there was more entailed here, something beyond mere appreciation, something Royce didn't want to examine or even acknowledge.

The very fact that he was taking pleasure from such a simple thing as a woman's height startled Royce. What did Megan's height have to do with anything? he asked himself, frowning in consternation. And the other underlying sensation . . . that didn't bear thinking about.

Dismissing his reaction and the unmentionable accompanying sensation as unimportant, Royce focused on Megan Delaney. Yes, she was tall, and she was unquestionably attractive, but at the moment every inch of her slender form was taut, visibly tense.

Royce repressed the sigh that rose to tighten his throat. Megan had gone through an extremely nasty experience, and it showed.

Royce recalled that, during her stuttered and disjointed recitation, he had been shaken by a startling conflict in the emotions tearing at his senses and sensibilities. His intellect had been outraged by the disclosure of the details of the attack on Megan. Assailed by fury, he had had to impose restraint on an overriding urge to jump up and dash from the room to search out, find and personally destroy the bastard who had terrorized her.

At one and the same time, his emotions had responded in an unprecedented way to a sudden and strong sense of attraction at the touch of her hand clinging to his.

Though Royce had pushed aside the unusual sensation then, as he did now, the memory lingered, a wisp of flotsam tossed about by an overwhelming wave of compassion.

Royce felt a deep, almost compulsive need to help her, in some way to ease the frightening mental and emotional aftereffects he knew she was suffering.

Frustration ate away at Royce like acid; Megan looked so damn vulnerable.

But how to help? The question had nagged at Royce for more than twenty-four hours. What could he do? He was a trained law-enforcement officer, but that certainly did not qualify him to deal with in-depth mental or emotional problems.

The only options that presented themselves to Royce seemed puny weapons of combat in relation to the magnitude of the inner battle tormenting Megan.

He could extend his hand for grasping. He could volunteer as a shield of law between her and the world at large. He could offer his strength as protection.

Puny, indeed, but...wait, Royce thought with sudden inspiration. The old adage of laughter being the best medicine had recently gained new, stronger credence. He had heard of physicians using it to treat a multitude of ills.

Maybe it would help, Royce mused. Surely, if doctors were employing it, it couldn't hurt.

Unnoticed as yet by the two women in the room, Royce stood silent, his eyes inventorying the look of Megan, comparing her beauty to the different yet equal beauty of the other woman, Dr. Virginia Hawk.

In point of fact, there really was no comparison, except that they were both beautiful women.

Whereas Megan had a mass of long, unruly-looking, fiery red hair, Virginia was a cool-looking blonde. And where Virginia was average in size, and maturely, enticingly curvaceous, Megan was tall, willowy, long-legged . . . and, in Royce's instant assessment, she looked more the model than the artist. Funny, he had never before been attracted to the lean, angular type.

But the attraction was certainly felt now, banished to the fringes of his awareness, but there just the same.

Royce didn't like it, but there wasn't a damn thing he could do about it.

"Oh, Sergeant, I didn't hear you come in."

Virginia Hawk's soft voice gently snared Royce's distracted attention.

"I just arrived a moment ago," he said, strolling into the room with a self-imposed casual air.

"Oh, good morning." Megan glanced around at the sound of his voice, revealing the bruised side of her face to his gaze. "I'm just about ready to go."

"No hurry. Take your time." Royce had difficulty keeping his voice steady, concealing the feelings bombarding him. The sight of the discolored bruises marring her lovely face reactivated conflicting feelings of burning anger and drenching tenderness. "Is there anything I can do to help?"

"No." Megan began to shake her head, but halted the movement at once, wincing in pain. "I just have to slip into my shoes, and we can leave."

"Okay." Royce shifted his gaze to the doctor. "Paperwork all cleared up?"

"Yes." Virginia smiled and nodded her head. "Megan is fine," she said, letting him know she had seen and understood his reaction to the other woman's appearance. "She has agreed to come in to my office next week for a follow-up visit, but it will simply be a checkup. I expect no adverse effects." Virginia hesitated, then added a qualification. "at least, no lasting physical effects."

Royce gave a brief, sharp nod of understanding. He had seen enough rape and attempted-rape cases to know that the major ramifications were primarily psychological in nature—and devastating in effect.

"I'm fine…really." Megan gave the doctor a bright, reassuring smile—too bright to be genuine, or reassuring. "But I promise I'll keep my appointment."

"Good, then get out of here," Virginia ordered, starting for the door. "I've got work to do."

A near-palpable tension entered the room the moment the doctor exited, leaving Royce and Megan alone together. In that instant, the average-size room seemed to shrink, becoming too small to contain both occupants.

Megan fidgeted with her blazer, which matched the stylish calf-length skirt she had worn to dinner with her friends. The skirt was now wrinkled and creased from her struggle with her unknown attacker.

"I…I want to get out of here," she said, in a harsh, wobbly voice. "I need a bath…desperately."

Royce understood that, as well. He knew, from experience, from talking with others who had gone through the same degrading horror Megan had suffered, the resultant feelings of being dirty, unclean, tainted.

"Then let's get moving." He didn't offer to help her as she shrugged into the blazer; he knew better. The last thing Megan wanted at this moment was to be touched, however impersonally, by a man, any man. Her grasping his hand yesterday had been an unconscious, instinctive reaction to reliving the fear-inducing incident. But that was then. This morning, she was fully conscious, aware and wary.

Megan preceded him from the room, the lithe gracefulness of her movements evident even through the tension tightening her tall form.

Royce felt his breath catch in his throat at the sight of the brave front Megan maintained. Admiration swelled inside him for her fierce display of independence, her attitude of calm and composure, despite the fine tremor quivering on her soft lips, in her slim fingers.

Wanting to help her, if only in a show of unstated support, Royce strode to her side, adjusting his long stride to hers, a silent buffer, there if she needed him.

Megan didn't say anything, but she slid a sidelong glance at him, a faint smile of comprehension and gratitude flickering briefly over her lips.

Dammit! Royce railed as her smile died a quick death, killed by the persistent tremor. And damn that bastard attacker to the deepest regions of hell.

"Which way?"

Royce blinked and glanced around, surprised to see that they were on the sidewalk outside the main entrance to the hospital, even more surprised by the realization that he had no actual recollection of traversing the corridors from point A to point B. All he could recall was moving beside her, ready, willing, to scoop her into his arms and run with her, should Megan give any sign of faltering, unable to continue on.

Pull it together, Wolfe, he advised himself, before you make an absolute jackass out of yourself. Megan gave every appearance of being the last woman in the world to lose control to the degree of needing to be bodily carried anywhere.

"Er...over there." He gestured vaguely toward the opposite curb. "The Pontiac Bonneville across the street."

"Nice car. I like that shimmery dark green color," Megan said, crossing the sidewalk. "Is it new?" She glanced right, then left, along the empty street before starting across.

"I've had it a couple of months." Royce shrugged. "It was new, but last year's model."

"Mine was brand-new." She heaved a sigh. "I had to wait for the exact shade of red I wanted. It was delivered to the dealer just three weeks ago."

"Too bad," he murmured in genuine sympathy.

Megan flicked a sidelong look at him. "The damage was extensive, wasn't it?"

"Yes," Royce said, knowing it was pointless to be less than truthful. "I checked with the mechanic at the garage yesterday afternoon. It's totaled, a write-off. The entire front end crumpled. We couldn't lift any fingerprints, because the door had wrinkled. I'm sorry."

"Why?" Though her shoulders slumped, Megan gave him a tired smile. "You didn't do it, I did."

Since there really was no argument against her assertion, Royce didn't bother attempting one. "You're alive," he said, offering her a compassionate smile as he unlocked and held open the passenger side door for her. Then, in silence, he circled around to the driver's side.

"Buckle up," he said without thinking, as he slid behind the steering wheel.

"I usually do." Megan's tone bordered on sarcasm. "I only ever forget when I'm in trauma."

"Happens a lot, does it?" Royce tried a teasing note, in hopes of defusing with a touch of humor the sudden tension humming inside the confines of the car.

Megan carefully connected the belt before slanting a wry look at him. "Trauma? Or—?

"Trauma," he quickly inserted, along with a grin.

She was quiet a moment, her expression pensive as she studied his eyes, his grin. Then, just as Royce could feel his face falling as flat as his obviously ill-timed levity, his mind frantically groping for something, anything to say, she gave him a weak smile in return.

"Yes," she said. "I suffer bouts of panic-inspired trauma with the approach of each and every assignment deadline."

"Ah..." he murmured, relieved that his earlier idea of applied laughter hadn't completely bombed, although in truth Megan wasn't laughing, she was just putting forth an effort to respond. "You're one of those artistic types who work close to the edge."

"Hardly artistic." Megan actually did manage a parody of laughter. "Truth be told, I'm one of those lazy types who screw around until the last minute, then pressure themselves into blind panic."

Royce found her candor refreshing, and amusing. He laughed with her. "A procrastinator, are you?"

"In spades." Megan's shoulders rippled in a half shrug, conveying a slight lessening of tension. "Always was." A smile of reminiscence tugged at her soft lips. "I always put off doing my homework, and every other chore, until I was threatened with dire consequences, like being grounded or having my allowance withheld. Drove my parents nuts, since they both are self-starters."

Encouraged by the easing of the tautness in her body and her stark expression, Royce said the first thing to come into his mind, in hopes of keeping her distracted.

"You could be describing my youngest brother," he said, chuckling. "When he was a kid, Jake had a positive talent for goofing off, and driving our parents nuts."

"Jake." Megan repeated the name, testing the sound of it. "I like the name. It sounds solid, somehow, not at all the name of a first-class goof-off."

"Oh, he's not anymore." Royce inserted the key and fired the engine. Then, since his distracting ploy appeared to be working, he quickly continued, "Jake goofed off for more than his share of years, but he's finally settled down, and settled in." He checked for oncoming traffic before pulling smoothly away from the curb.

"In what way?" Megan had turned sideways in her seat to look at him, and she sounded genuinely interested in hearing about the trials and tribulations the Wolfe clan had endured through the maturing period of the youngest of the brood.

Royce was only too happy to oblige. Anything to keep her mind occupied, away from the memory of her ordeal. "After kicking around the country for a lot of years, Jake came home, attended the police academy, then took a job with the hometown police force." Drawing the car to a halt at a stop sign, he turned to smile at her. "Mom tells me that Jake has turned out to be a damn good cop. As good as all the others in the family."

Megan arched delicate auburn eyebrows. "There's more than you and Jake? Cops, I mean."

Royce laughed as he set the car in motion again. "A bunch... or at least there were. Following the law is a family tradition, dating back over a hundred years. Even as we speak, there are four—count 'em, four— Wolfe men working in law enforcement."

"All of you?" She blinked in astonishment.

"Yeah. A real hoot, huh?"

"And a holler," she drawled. "Turn right at the next intersection."

"I know." Royce slanted a wry glance at her. "I'm a cop, remember? I know the district."

"I'm impressed."

"I seriously doubt it."

Megan laughed, a free-floating sound that lifted Royce's spirits. The fact that she looked both relaxed and comfortable in the plush seat was an added bonus.

"What branch of law enforcement are the other two Wolfe men in?" She flashed Royce a quick grin. "Wolfe men . . . conjures up images of hairy faces and hands, and sudden claws, and long, ululating cries to the full moon."

Royce nearly lost it. Gripping the wheel, he choked back a roar of laughter, and shook his head in helpless amusement. Megan Delaney was proving to be a real trip. Her display of humor after the ordeal she had been through spoke volumes about her inner strength.

Royce liked what he heard; and he liked her. The liking enhanced the attraction he felt for her. That, he didn't particularly appreciate; Royce wasn't heavily into frustration, emotional or otherwise.

He frowned.

"You've forgotten?"

"What?" Royce shot a scowling look at her.

"What branch of law enforcement your brothers are in?" she said, scowling back at him.

"Oh." Royce offered a sheepish smile; she returned it with a dry look. "Well, Eric—he's the third son—followed our father into the Philadelphia police force. He's currently undercover with the narcotics division. And big brother Cameron is a special agent for the FBI."

Megan frowned in concentration. "That means that Cameron's the oldest, right?"

"Right. The Lone Wolfe."

"That's his code name?"

"Nah." Royce laughed. "That's the moniker his friends and fellow agents hung on him a couple or so years ago."

"Self-contained, is he?" she asked. "All of an individual piece?"

"Yeah." Royce rewarded her with an admiring glance. "That's very good . . . apt."

"Here's the driveway," Megan said, taking evident pleasure from his compliment. She indicated the drive with a fluttery hand motion. "It's a sharp turn."

"No kidding, Dick Tracy," he muttered, flicking a glance into the rearview mirror before hanging a hard right.

She gave him a puzzled look. "What?"

"Nothing." Royce shrugged, and flashed another grin at her. "Mumbling to myself."

"Uh-huh," she responded, again as dry as dust.

Located a little way beyond the limits of Conifer, the split-level house of natural stone and wood was set like a gem into the tree-dotted landscape, secluded yet not isolated from several surrounding properties.

"Pretty," he observed, bringing the car to a stop in front of the house.

"Yes," Megan softly agreed. "When my parents had it constructed twenty-five years ago, it was the only house in the area. They've picked up a few neighbors since then."

"So I see." Royce set the hand brake. "Close, but not too close. How big is the lot?"

"Two and a half acres." Megan smiled, and reached for the door release. "Which equates to a whole lot of mowing for my father." She shoved the door open and slid her legs out, then hesitated on the edge of the bucket seat. "Er...would you like a cup of coffee?"

"Sure," Royce said at once, picking up on the sudden note of uncertainty in her voice. The story was written plain as day on her face. She was trying hard to conceal it, but the tension was back, riddling her taut form, terrorizing her mind, making her fear entering the house alone.

"I'd offer you lunch..." she said, stepping from the car and waiting for him to join her before heading for the front door. "But I can't recall what I have in the house to eat." She gave a shaky-sounding laugh. "Strange, I've only been away two nights, and yet it seems so much longer."

"Stuff happens," Royce murmured.

"Yeah." Megan sighed; her fingers trembled as she fumbled the key into the lock. "Mind-bending stuff."

"It'll fade." His voice held just the right note of authority... Royce hoped.

"When?" For all the demand in her tone, a tremor of fear and uncertainty filtered through, delivering a blow to his emotions. Flinging the door open, she strode inside, then whirled to confront him as he followed her into the small flagstone foyer. "A month? A year? Ten years?"

"Stay calm, Megan," he said, soothingly, softly, hurting for her, and for himself, for not having met her before a brainless, violence-prone jerk messed up her mind.

"Calm. Yes." She took a deep breath. Tried a smile. Missed it. Sank her teeth into her lower lip. Shook her head. "Oh, hell!" Blinking furiously against the sudden brightness in her eyes, she spun around and dashed away, down a short hallway, heading toward the rear of the house. "I'll... I'll make the coffee."

Wanting to go to her, to comfort her, yet knowing he should not, Royce stood in the middle of the foyer, controlling himself, while giving her time to gather her own control.

Silently counting off the seconds, he glanced around, taking inventory of his surroundings.

To his right, along the hallway, were two closed doors. Bedrooms? Royce wondered, shrugging. To his left, the hallway was open, railed with intricate wrought iron. Three half-moon-shaped flagstone steps descended into a spacious living room, brightly illuminated by the sunlight pouring through two oversize picture windows, one facing the front of the house, one facing the side.

The living room was open-ended, flowing into the dining room. The decor was country, in primary colors—forest, bark brown and Williamsburg blue. The furniture was high-backed, with plump cushions, a mute invitation to rest and relaxation.

Royce liked it; it reminded him of home.

Three minutes had elapsed, by his silent figuring. Drawing a breath, he struck out, trailing in Megan's wake.

She was standing at the kitchen counter, staring fixedly at the water trickling through the grounds basket into the glass pot of an automatic coffeemaker.

"Okay now?" Royce kept his voice low, unobtrusive.

Megan exhaled a ragged-sounding sigh. "Yes... but..." She turned to ricochet a glance off him. "I..." She gulped in a breath. "I suppose it's silly, but I must have a shower," she said, rushing on, "and I'm afraid of being here, in the house, alone." She lifted fear-darkened eyes to his. "Would you mind very much having your coffee alone? Staying until I'm finished?"

Royce felt her imploring look to the depths of his heart and mind. "Not at all," he said, in a soft, yet reassuring voice. "I don't start work till three."

"Thank you." Megan lowered her gaze, swallowed, then glanced up at him once more. "The coffee's almost done. Help yourself. There're cups in the cabinet." She walked toward him, a silent plea in her eyes for him to step aside so that she wouldn't have to brush against him as she passed.

"I'll find them." Royce stepped aside, giving her space. "I promise not to drink it all."

"Thank you." A fleeting smile touched her lips. "I, uh, may be awhile. If you get hungry, feel free to rummage in the cabinets and fridge for sustenance."

"Okay, thanks. Can I get something for you?"

Megan hesitated, hovering in the doorway, obviously anxious to escape, yet also obviously appreciative of his offer of help. "I'm not really hungry right now. Maybe later. But thanks, anyway," she said. Then she scurried through the doorway and back along the hall to the first door inside the entrance.

Royce watched her until the door closed behind her. There came the faint but definite sound of the lock clicking into place. Heaving a sigh, he turned to glance around the room.

He liked the kitchen even more than the living room, but then, that wasn't too surprising—Royce was a kitchen person. And this particular kitchen held definite appeal.

Done in earth tones of terra-cotta and sage, with bright splashes of pumpkin and honey-brown, the room was warm and homey. A large, solid-looking round table was placed in front of a wide window overlooking the side yard. Four armed captain's chairs circled the table.

Finding a cup in the cabinet above the coffeemaker, Royce filled it with the steaming brew and carried it to the table. He found milk in the double-door refrigerator, sniffed it, then tipped a quick dollop into his coffee.

Then, sliding a chair away from the table, he settled into the curved, padded seat, stretched out his legs and sipped at the hot liquid, prepared to wait as long as it took for Megan to decide she was once again clean.

Royce's stomach grumbled a demand for sustenance on his third trip from the table to the coffeepot. He sent a brooding look through the doorway and along the hall. The bedroom door Megan had disappeared behind remained shut. He switched his gaze to the refrigerator, and his expression grew contemplative.

Should he or shouldn't he?

Why not? He *had* been invited to browse.

Pulling the double doors apart, Royce took stock of the freezer section. Vegetables, microwave dinners, individually wrapped and labeled packages of meat.

He shook his head. Too heavy for lunch.

Closing the door, he turned his attention to the contents of the other, bigger side. The wire shelves contained much more promising fare. There were cartons of milk, both whole and low-fat. Other cartons of juices—tomato, orange and grapefruit. Bottles of springwater bearing a French label. On the shelf below were packets of luncheon meats and sliced white

American cheese, jars of pickles, olives, mustard, mayonnaise, ketchup and horseradish.

Things were looking up.

Royce bent to peer at the lower shelf. Not quite as interesting. The covered containers bore the definite appearance of leftovers.

Forget that.

There were two drawers beneath the bottom shelf. Royce slid out the first one. Now we're getting somewhere, he thought, identifying lettuce, tomatoes, celery, and a dark green bunch of parsley. He removed all but the last, leaving the dark green bunch all on its lonesome.

Depositing the veggies on the table, he returned to the fridge to investigate the bottom drawer. Oranges, grapefruit, kiwi fruit, seedless green grapes, and a small basket of fresh California strawberries. Yum, yum....

Royce found an assortment of bottled salad dressings on a narrow shelf on the door and a small can of white tuna in one of the cabinets above the countertop.

He was in business.

Twenty-odd minutes later, Royce stepped back from the counter to admire the results of his industrious labor. A smug smile of satisfaction played over his lips as he shifted his gaze from the large wooden bowl piled high with crisp salad sprinkled with pieces of white tuna to a smaller glass bowl, colorful with its tossed assortment of fresh fruits.

Okay. What now? Frowning, Royce shot another look the length of the hallway; the bedroom door remained shut.

Beginning to wonder if he should go rap on the door, if only to make sure Megan hadn't drowned herself, he sighed and began opening cabinet doors again, searching out dishes and glassware to set the table for two—just in case Megan's appetite was awakened by his offering.

When the table was ready, Royce hunted up the ground coffee and started a fresh pot of coffee. He was staring at the liquid trickling from the basket into the pot in the exact same manner Megan had been earlier, when her quiet voice broke through his concerned reverie.

"You have been busy, haven't you?"

Relief shuddered through Royce. Controlling his expression, he slowly turned around.

The sight of her ripped the breath from his throat.

Megan was standing in the doorway, looking beautiful enough to stop rush-hour traffic. And yet her choice of attire could only be called casual in the extreme.

Soft-looking faded jeans embraced her slender hips and long legs. Crumpled pink satin ballerina slippers encased her narrow feet. An oversize baggy sweatshirt emblazoned with the words Kutztown State concealed her breasts.

Her face looked fresh-scrubbed, pale, devoid of artifice; not so much as a hint of blush, lip gloss or eye shadow had been applied to enhance her colorless skin.

In sharp and blazing contrast, her long mane of fiery hair gave the appearance of a living flame, framing her face and tumbling in springy spiral curls around her shoulders and halfway down her back.

Stunned, Royce could barely breathe, never mind speak. Still, he gave it a shot.

"Uh, I, uh, yeah..." He moved his hand in an absent way, indicating the table. "I made lunch."

"I see." Megan's somber gaze followed his hand. "Everything looks good, appetizing."

Inordinately pleased by her mild approval, Royce moved his shoulders in a dismissive shrug. "It's only tossed salad and mixed fruit."

"But you took the time and trouble to do it... for me." She swallowed with visible difficulty. "I...I..." She broke off to swallow again. "Thank you, Royce. You're a nice man." A tiny, faintly bitter smile feathered her lips. "And right now I'm inclined to believe there aren't an awful lot of nice men littering the ground."

What could he say? Royce asked himself. How could he refute her new, hard-earned belief? She had suffered the debasement of a man attempting to force himself on her. In his opinion, she was justified in her need to withdraw, to wrap herself within the folds of a cloak of detachment from all things male.

"Ah, Megan..." he murmured, heaving a defeated sounding sigh. "Trite as I know it is, there is, nevertheless, truth to the saying that it will pass in time."

"Oh, God! I hope so!" she said in a soft, fervent cry. "Because I hate the fragile, helpless, frightened way I'm feeling now!"

Resisting an urgent impulse to go to her, pull her into the safe, protective haven of his arms, Royce moved in stiff-legged strides to the table.

"Come, eat something," he implored her, sliding a chair away from the table invitingly. "Things always look better on a full stomach than on an empty one."

Megan arched one auburn eyebrow. "You're just full of homespun wisdom, aren't you?" she chided.

"That's me, your friendly old philosopher." He made a low, sweeping bow, trying to lighten the atmosphere. "Won't you join me for lunch?"

"I'm really not hungry," Megan said, taking a cautious step toward him.

"Then how about joining me while I have lunch?" Royce pleaded, plaintively, pathetically. "Like most bachelors, I eat alone most of the time. It gets... lonely."

His tone, combined with the sorrowful expression he pulled, drew a small but real smile from her. Heaving an exaggerated sigh, she crossed the room to accept the chair he still held in readiness for her.

"You're a fraud, Sergeant," she said accusingly, slipping onto the chair, being careful not to touch him. "A sham," she continued, with less strain, when he moved to the chair opposite her. "You're not a big bad Wolfe at all."

The response that sprang into his mind was triggered by a remark Megan had made earlier, while they were still in the car, discussing his family. Without thinking, he allowed it to flow softly from his lips.

"Don't bet on it, Megan. Wanna hear my ululating full-moon howl?"

Four

Laughter erupted from Megan's throat. She couldn't help it. Even feeling shaky, vulnerable to the point of fragility, she just could not contain a burst of appreciative laughter.

Royce slanted a sly, assessing look at her.

He had done it on purpose, Megan suddenly realized. Royce had deliberately tossed the wry remark at her. The look of him, the light dancing in the depths of his incredibly blue eyes, told her all she needed to know for now about the man seated, lounging in a deceptive pose of laziness, opposite her. He had wanted to alleviate her feelings of anxiety and strain, ease the tension tearing at her, by making her laugh.

What a thoroughly decent man.

The evaluation of him startled Megan, considering her rather low opinion of the male species in general at this particular time.

But this man was different, she mused, absently helping herself to a good-size portion of salad.

Her eyes flickered upward to his face, then quickly away again as another equally startling thought popped into her head. Royce was not only different from that hulking, grunting beast who had attacked her, Royce was different from any other man she had ever met.

The difference was unrelated to looks; even though Royce was one very good-looking man. Megan knew many good-looking, even downright handsome, men. And it had little to do with his size, which was considerable, imposing.

No, Megan mused, raising her salad fork to her mouth. The difference lay in the man himself, his personality, the innate decent character traits slowly being revealed to her. Royce Wolfe was a good man, a good person who genuinely cared about people. Megan would unhesitatingly have wagered her last dollar on it.

Having someone care about the ordeal she had been through, the resulting trauma she now had to deal with, consoled Megan more than she would have believed possible. The knotted feeling in her stomach relaxed, simply because he was there, caring, lending a sense of security.

He was staring at her. Though she kept her gaze
lowered to the luncheon plate, and the salad she had
begun eating without conscious intent, Megan could
sense, feel, Royce's pensive and probing stare upon
her.

What was he watching for, waiting for?

Was Royce expecting her to crumple into a heap and
wail like a lost or injured child?

Megan swallowed down a small piece of lettuce that
had caught, then stuck, in her throat.

She very easily could let loose and cry like an aban-
doned child, simply because that was precisely what
she longed to do. More than wail, though, she wanted
to scream at the top of her voice, rant and rave, rail
against the vagaries of a fate that had placed her in
that particular parking lot at that particular time.

Megan took another bite of salad and chewed de-
terminedly. She didn't taste the delicate flavor of the
tuna, the crispness of the vegetables, or the creami-
ness of the ranch dressing.

What good would screaming and ranting do her,
anyway? Would it change her situation? Would it wipe
from her memory the choking fear she had felt, the
fear that still curled around the edges of her mind?
Would it return her to the confident, carefree frame of
mind she had enjoyed, taken for granted before the
attack?

No. No. No.

Nothing would ever be the same. *She* would never be the same. Megan knew it, and she resented the knowledge.

She had done nothing, nothing, to encourage an attack. How dare that hulking bastard, how dare any person take it into his maggoty mind to make a victim of her or any other human being?

"Megan?"

Megan shuddered at the softly intrusive sound of Royce's voice. A great deal of effort was required on her part to keep from snarling in response.

"What?"

"Hey, c'mon, calm down," Royce said, raising his hands in a sign of surrender. "I'm friendly, remember?"

"Sorry." Megan sighed, and gave him a faint smile. "I was all caught up in my thoughts."

"Bad, huh?"

"Yeah."

"Yeah," he echoed, exhaling harshly. "I want to tell you to put it out of your mind, but I know that's one whole hell of a lot easier said than done."

"Yes, it is." Her smile took on a self-deprecating slant. "It's at times like this that we realize how very trite we tend to be when offering our unsolicited advice to others." Megan sighed again. "I'm afraid that I'm as guilty of doing so as everyone else. Sad, isn't it?"

"Don't go down."

Megan blinked. "I beg your pardon?"

"You're in a downward spiral," Royce explained, his glittering eyes piercing hers. "I can hear it in your voice, see it in your face. I've witnessed it before, that mental lure into depression. Fight it, Megan."

Megan glanced away from him, his intensity. She blinked again, this time not in confusion, but against a hot rush of moisture to her eyes. "As I believe you mentioned," she murmured, "it's easier said than done."

"But it can be done." His voice was hard, adamant. "Get help if necessary, from Dr. Hawk, or your pastor, if you have one, or maybe a close friend, but fight, fight with every atom of resistance you possess. *Don't let him win.*"

The very strength of his voice, of his command, drew her gaze back to his sternly set features, and then to the hand he had extended across the table to her, palm up, in exactly the same way he had in the hospital.

Get help. Fight. His command spun through her head, sparking corollary, comforting thoughts.

With the simple act of offering her his hand, Royce was silently offering his help, offering his strength, offering to fight with her, beside her.

Megan's throat closed around an emotional lump.

Had she judged Royce Wolfe decent? she thought, reaching for his proffered hand. *Decent* seemed much too mild a term to apply in defining the man.

Megan's palm slid onto his; it was warm, not smooth, as she might have expected of the hand of a desk jockey, but rough, callused, the hand of a man familiar with hard physical work. It was oddly reassuring, the rough feel of that hand.

Megan swallowed to relieve the tightness, and when that didn't work, she cleared her throat of the tear-congealed emotional lump.

"I..." She cast a quick glance at him, and was nearly undone by the look of tenderness that had eased the stern set of his features. "Thank you."

"Hey, you're welcome." Royce's voice was low, soothing, and held a hint of entreaty. "How 'bout some fruit?"

Fruit? Megan frowned and looked at her plate. It was empty. When had she eaten the last of her salad? She shook her head to clear the cobwebs of confusion, cast another look at him, and once again had to smile.

"Okay, Sergeant Perceptive," she agreed on a sigh, "let's have some fruit."

Royce grinned, and the room appeared to brighten considerably. "Awright..." he said, releasing her hand, then shoving his chair back and springing to his feet. "You dish up the fruit, and I'll pour the coffee."

The house was quiet, too quiet, after Royce left to go to work. At loose ends, Megan wandered from room to room, glancing at everything, each carefully selected piece of furniture, each accent piece her mother had purchased after days, sometimes weeks,

of shopping for just the right colors, the perfect dec-
orative items. Since her mother's taste was excellent,
the decor was both aesthetically appealing and comfortable.

The beauty and ambience were lost on Megan in her
present frame of mind. Although she looked, she did
not see the warmth, the welcome. All she saw was the
emptiness.

She was alone.

It scared her sick.

Fight.

The echoing sound of Royce's voice rang so clear in
Megan's mind, she jumped and whirled around, expecting to see him standing in the doorway, his right
hand extended in an unstated offer of help.

He wasn't there.

But the subconscious memory echo had served its
purpose. Megan's vision cleared. She was home. She
was safe. And she would be damned if she'd allow
herself to tumble into that downward spiral into depression Royce had warned her against.

Squaring her shoulders, Megan strode from the living room to her bedroom, and straight to the work
area, in a corner between two oversize windows. She
trailed her hand along the edge of her drafting table set
at an angle to the large desk beneath one window.
Glancing aside, she stared into the black screen of her
computer, on which she created graphic designs for
certain assignments.

But Megan was not using the computer for her current assignment. She was working in the medium of her first love, illustrative painting, with real paints and real brushes and the very real odors that went with it.

Megan respected the computer, and its mind-boggling capabilities, and so she gave it a quick nod of recognition. It was then that she noticed the tiny red light on the answering machine next to the telephone on the corner of the desk. She rewound the tape and pressed the play button. The first message was from the friend she had dined with Friday night.

"Hi, Meg, it's Julie, as if you didn't know." Julie's tinkling laughter brought a sad smile to Megan's lips. "It's Saturday morning, 10:35," she went on, "and I suppose you're off shopping or something."

Or something, Megan thought, suppressing a shudder spawned by the memory of her emotional display while relating the events of her ordeal to Royce in the hospital Saturday morning.

"...wonderful seeing you again..." Julie was going on, recapturing Megan's attention. "Cliff and I have really missed your company and smiling face since you moved back here, but we do understand how you might feel safer here than living alone in New York."

Safer! Megan groaned. The machine beeped and Julie's voice was cut off. Seconds later, the beep sounded again, and Julie was back, laughter in her voice.

"It's me again. Meg, I'm gonna have to run. Clifford is bugging me to get moving. We're off on a hike into the hills— How lucky can one woman get? If I don't get a chance to talk to you before we leave tomorrow, I'll give you a buzz one day next week. See ya."

"See ya," Megan murmured, envisioning her friend's dear pixie face, her smiling eyes. "And please be careful, both of you. There's danger in those hills," she went on in a choked whisper, as a hulking form intruded on her vision.

Caught up once again in the memory of that violent man, that terrifying experience, Megan began to shiver. Tears welled up to sting her eyes and clog her throat. A moan of protest was torn from the depths of her chest, and she shook her head to dispel the vision, the memory.

"Royce." Megan was unaware of whimpering his name aloud, of crying out for his stabilizing presence, the physical strength of his hand, the psychological strength of his being.

He was not there to rescue her. The answering machine responded in his stead. It beeped, then played another message, this one from her current employer—and onetime would-be lover—Jefferson Clarke, Jr. Though Megan had never been able to respond on an emotional level to Jeff, he had continued to utilize her professional talents, and they had developed an abiding friendship.

Jefferson held the title of associate publisher with Clarke and Clarke, Inc., father-and-son publishers of a quarterly magazine with a chic and savvy format, geared for the young—and not-so-young—up-and-coming executive.

"Megan, I'm waiting for the illustrations that were supposed to be on my desk last week," he said, not unkindly. "Can I look for them anytime soon?"

The sound of Jeff's chiding voice broke through the haze of remembered fear gripping Megan. She smiled faintly and sniffed as the machine issued a double beep, indicating the end of her messages. Raising her hand, she swiped the film of tears from her eyes before erasing the tape and resetting the machine.

Should she give Jeff a call, explain the situation, and the subsequent psychological and emotional effects? Megan mused, drawing in deep, shuddering breaths. Knowing Jeff, she felt certain that he would react to her ordeal with both compassion and understanding, and very likely offer her a deadline extension, possibly even the option of scrapping the project. In all likelihood, Jeff might go so far as offering to come to Conifer to be with her for a while, to give her moral support.

But she *had* moral support, right here in Conifer.

Of course, the thought conjured up an image of Royce, and the image sparked an attendant vision, demanding a comparison between the two men.

Megan frowned as she mentally examined the pictures filling her mind. In truth, there really was no comparison.

Jefferson Clarke was a bit taller than average, a tad taller than Megan herself. He had a dark olive complexion, dark eyes and hair. His build was slender, elegant, a living, breathing reflection of the conventional concept of the aristocrat. In other words, Jeff was the complete opposite of the very tall, muscular, sun-kissed, earthy Royce Wolfe.

It wasn't until that instant that Megan realized that she preferred earthy to aristocratic.

Preferred? Megan's frown deepened. The connotations inherent in the word gave her pause. At the moment, under her present circumstances, her preference in regard to men should have been the absolute last thing to spring to her mind.

Yet, there it was, nudged to the forefront of her consciousness by the persistent image of Royce's visage confronting her, stirring a flicker of feminine interest to life inside her.

A shiver skipped down Megan's spine, a shiver born more from excitement than from fear.

Ridiculous. Megan moved her head in another hard shake, dislodging the visions of both men. Then a faint smile of gratitude curved her lips as the thought occurred that, in point of fact, the two images had superseded that of her frightening attacker—and all because of a phone message.

Sending a silent but heartfelt thanks to Jefferson Clarke for saving her from herself, from surrendering to fear, she turned away from the desk to stare lovingly at the work in progress attached to her table.

Megan had worked on numerous projects for Clarke and Clarke since going free-lance. She enjoyed working with the Clarkes, father and son, and the bright, energetic and imaginative employees of the company, and she hoped to continue working with them in the future.

But she wouldn't have a prayer of seeing her hopes realized if she cringed in a corner. She had an assignment to complete, and she was already over deadline, as Jeff had pointedly reminded her via her answering machine.

Ever since she first took a colored pencil to drawing paper at the age of five, Megan had been able to lose herself in her imagination, and the creations it conjured up. Her lips compressed into a thin line of determination to fight backsliding with her strongest weapon, Megan slid onto the stool in front of the table.

It was time for all good little illustrators to cut through the emotional crap and get down to business.

It was a long workday, and it was only a little more than half over.

Royce shot a glance at the office wall clock and suppressed a sigh. The hands stood at 8:37.

It had been dark outside for several hours now. How was Megan handling the nighttime hours?

The thought directed his gaze to the phone. Royce lifted his hand, then let it drop to the desktop again.

He wanted to call Megan, hear her voice assuring him that she was all right.

Of course she was all right, he chided himself, closing the folder on the desk in front of him. He slid the folder into the out basket and reached into the in basket for another one. He opened the folder and frowned at the top sheet of paper. The information contained on the page merged into wavy lines of seeming gibberish.

Frustrated, impatient, unsettled, Royce pushed the file aside and sat back in his chair, one foot tapping a rhythmic tattoo on the tile floor.

At the rate he was moving, he mused, he'd be lucky to get halfway through the stack in the in basket by quitting time.

And it was not his style. Royce had a reputation for dedication to detail, and for completing his work duties ahead of schedule. His fellow officers loved ribbing him about being a workaholic cop.

Royce didn't mind the flak, because he knew it was just that, good-natured flak. Besides, in all honesty, he knew there was more than a little truth to their claim. He *was* something of a workaholic. He was also a good cop.

But, at that precise moment, Royce felt anything but either. He felt helpless and ineffectual.

Yet, like it or not, there wasn't a whole lot Royce could do about the situation. He had already talked to the officer investigating the attack on Megan. And Stew Javorsky had sounded as frustrated as Royce felt.

"Sorry, Sarge, but there's not much to report," Stew had said, his expression woeful. "Nobody saw anything. Nobody heard anything. There have been no other reports or complaints of similar occurrences." He'd heaved a sigh. "And there isn't even a heck of a lot to go on. I mean, the description—'large, hulking and rough-voiced'—isn't exactly...exact."

"I know." Royce had moved his wide shoulders in a helpless shrug. "I'm hoping Miss Delaney will recall more details of the man's appearance when the initial shock and trauma wear off."

"Wouldn't hurt," Stew had agreed dryly. "Meanwhile, I'll keep you informed if anything should turn up."

Royce had thanked Stew, then tried to bury his frustration and impatience in his work.

That had been hours ago, and his diversionary ploy had produced only minor results.

Should he just go ahead and call her?

Royce scowled as he mulled over the question, unwilling to admit, even to himself, that there was an aching need expanding inside him just to hear the sound of her voice. Yet, whether or not he was willing to admit to it, the attraction to Megan that he had initially experienced had been gaining strength and momentum ever since she grasped his hand and hung on as if for dear life, yesterday morning in the hospital.

But the really telling incident had happened several hours ago, when Megan had once again placed her hand in his.

Royce had been hard-pressed to keep from jolting in reaction to the feel of her soft palm gliding onto his. A confusing and unfamiliar tingling sensation of applied heat had flashed from his palm to the outer reaches of his body.

Concealing his reaction from Megan had taxed every ounce of control Royce possessed.

Both shocked and baffled by the intensity of the excitement dancing along his nerve endings from their connecting palms, Royce had been forced to grit his teeth to squash an urgent impulse to caress the back of her hand, test the texture of her soft skin with his long fingers.

Against all reason, against all decency, Royce wanted Megan.

It was stupid.

It was reprehensible.

It was there, the wanting, burning in the core of his body, the depths of his mind.

Damn his soul, his maleness, his physical responses.

Although Royce had continued to damn anything and everything he could think of about himself, as a man, as a person, his feelings had not changed one iota.

He wanted Megan.

There was only one thing Royce wanted more than to be with Megan: He wanted her safe.

Without conscious direction, his hand again moved toward the phone. Stopping himself short, Royce drew his hand back and laid it flat on the desktop.

She was all right. Of course she was all right. He'd have heard if she wasn't. Hadn't he made a point of having her promise to call the barracks, call him, if there were any incidents, or anything at all, regardless how seemingly unimportant, out of the ordinary?

He had. Before leaving her, Royce had insisted Megan make that promise to him.

And since Megan hadn't called, he had to assume she was perfectly fine, secure in the safety of her parents' home.

Employing an old phrase his mother had chided her sons with whenever they appeared to be getting over-anxious about anything, Royce called himself a worrywart, opened the folder in front of him and told himself to get with the program.

Nevertheless, before focusing his full attention on his work, Royce made an anxiety-easing promise to himself.

He shot another glance at the wall clock and stifled a curse of impatience.

Now the hands stood at 8:57. He had two and a half hours to get through before he could leave, but then he'd be out of there, intent on carrying out his promise.

When his shift was over, and before going home, Royce had decided, he'd make a swing by Megan's place . . . just to check out the situation for his own satisfaction.

Five

Megan started awake at the jarring sound of the doorbell. Disoriented, she glanced around, heart pounding, nerves jangling, adrenaline surging through her bloodstream. The bell sounded again, and she jolted upright, out of the chair.

Who—? Megan shuddered as an image of a large, hulking, rough-voiced man filled her mind.

She was alone in the house, and it was late. How late? Megan shot a look at the gleaming sunburst clock on the wall above the fireplace mantel.

The clock read 12:05.

The bell pealed once more, followed by the unmistakable sound of the doorknob being turned.

Megan froze. Dear heaven! Was it him? she thought frantically. Was it that awful man, trying to get at her to finish what he had started Friday night?

Panic crawled into her stomach, making her feel physically sick, weak-kneed, terrified.

But wait! Think.

The attacker didn't know her name...did he? Megan frowned in concentration. Into her mind stole the faint echo of his voice, nasty-sounding, at first calling a generic "lady," then, as she struggled, fought him, snarling a guttural command: "Be still, you crazy bitch."

No, Megan reasoned, he probably didn't know her name. Therefore, he couldn't very likely know where she lived, she thought, exhaling a whooshing sigh of relief that caught in her throat when another summons trilled from the doorbell.

Panic flared anew, causing a flutter inside her chest, but a faint voice inside her mind called for deeper thought.

Obeying the order from her subconscious, Megan drew in deep, calming breaths, and applied her mind to more reasoned, rational contemplation, backtracking, then following the trail of her earlier actions.

Losing track of the passage of time, Megan had labored over her worktable until after nine, and wouldn't have quit then if not for a nagging and painful cramping in her lower back. Weariness had slammed into her when she slid from the stool and stepped away from the table.

Rubbing the base of her spine, Megan had stood still for a moment, gathering the dregs of her strength. A rumble of hunger from her empty stomach had finally propelled her from her bedroom on rubbery legs.

Leaving the lights burning in her bedroom, Megan had turned on the lights in each successive room she entered. In the kitchen, she'd fixed a quick meal consisting of a sandwich and a glass of skim milk.

It was while she methodically chewed the tasteless sandwich that Megan had been swamped by an overwhelming need to talk to her mother. She'd rushed to the wall phone, and been reaching for the receiver before she remembered that her mother, her parents, were halfway around the world, on a ship on the high seas, midway between ports of call.

The realization that she could not bolster her flagging spirits with the comforting sound of her mother's voice had drained the last of Megan's meager supply of energy.

Forgetting the remains of her slapped-together supper, and again leaving the bright overhead kitchen light on, she'd wandered into the living room, flicking on the swag light above the dining room table, the wall sconces, and then every table and floor lamp in the living room.

After securely closing the drapes over the wide living room windows, Megan had sunk into her father's favorite, deeply cushioned recliner and shut her eyes . . . just to rest for a few minutes.

She had been lost to the world within seconds.

That had been over two hours ago. Now, the last foggy wisps of sleep banished from her mind, Megan stood, taut and wary, her brain working at near full capacity.

Except for the draped windows in the living room, the house was ablaze with lights, indicating to any and all friends, neighbors and passersby that somebody was not only at home, but awake and aware.

Yet how many friends, neighbors or passersby came visiting after twelve o'clock at night?

Megan went stiff as a board as the doorbell trilled again, hard, quick, as if from the impatient stab of a finger stiffened by anger.

Get a grip, Megan told herself, fighting for all she was worth against paralyzing terror. Even if the attacker had somehow gotten her name and address, would a potential rapist announce himself by ringing the doorbell?

Not hardly, Megan chided herself bracingly, exhaling another whooshing breath of relief.

The bell rang yet again, immediately followed by a rapping tattoo against the wood-encased steel panel and a low-pitched, sharply concerned call.

"Megan, are you in there? Are you all right?"

Royce!

As his name exploded inside her mind, Megan was off and running to the door.

"I'm here!" she answered, raising her voice in case he had turned away. "Don't leave!" she cried, mentally cursing as she fumbled with the security lock.

"I had no intention—" the lock clicked, and she swung open the door "—of leaving."

Sergeant Royce Wolfe did not look like a very happy man. In point of fact, decked out in his smart state police uniform, he looked intimidating as hell.

Megan thought he was the best-looking thing she had seen in . . . well, in forever.

"You having a party or something?" Royce asked in a terse, clipped voice.

"A party?" Megan blinked. "Of course not! Why in the world would you think that?"

"You want an immediate answer," he fairly growled, "or may I come in out of the rain?"

"Oh! It's raining again." Megan backed away from the doorway. "I didn't know. Come on in."

"Thanks." Royce stepped past her into the flagged foyer, and only then did she notice the damp patches on the shoulders of his uniform jacket. "It's more a heavy mist than a rainfall," he said, raising his hand to remove his stiff-brimmed hat. "But the temperature's dropping, and it's beginning to freeze on the ground." He passed the hat to her.

"Don't you have a slicker or something for protection?" Megan asked, watching as he unfastened the buttons on his jacket. "And I thought you guys were issued plastic thingies to cover your hats." She ran her hand over the stiff, damp brim.

"Thingies?" The light of anger in Royce's glittering blue eyes gave way to a gleam of amusement.

"You know what I mean," she retorted, reaching for the jacket as he shrugged out of it.

"Yeah, I know what you mean." Royce surrendered the jacket to her, along with a smile. "The *thingie* is in its bag, which is in the car, on the seat, beneath the slicker."

"Oh." Megan stood there, holding his jacket and staring at him in bewildered admiration.

In the gray police-issue shirt and pants, Royce was a sight to behold. Of course, Megan mused, bemused, at least in his case, the smart-looking dark gray uniform did not make the man. Quite the contrary. With his so-tall, muscularly trim physique and his sharp-featured, sun-kissed good looks, Royce most decidedly made the uniform.

He'd said something.

"Huh?" Megan shook herself out of distraction and into awareness.

"I asked if you were feeling all right."

"Yes, fine," she said. "Why do you ask?"

"Because you're staring at me," he answered, frowning. "And you've got a strange look on your face."

"Oh." Upset with herself for becoming distracted by his masculine appeal, Megan raked a hand through her already tousled hair, and searched her mind for an intelligent response. "Really?" was all she could come up with, which sounded pretty lame, even to her own ears.

"Yes, really," Royce replied. "Something bothering you? Something about me, I mean?"

"Oh, no," she told him, giving a sharp shake of her head to reinforce her falsehood. "I had dozed off on the recliner in the living room, you see," she babbled. "The doorbell startled me, and I guess I'm still not quite awake yet."

"Uh-huh," he murmured, eyeing her speculatively. Then, his voice taking on a note of understanding, he asked, "You afraid to go to bed?"

"Afraid?" Megan repeated, bristling at the mere suggestion of a lack of inner fortitude...even if it did happen to be true. "Why would you think that I'm afraid?"

"Elementary, my dear Megan," Royce said, dryly paraphrasing a famous fictional detective. "Your falling asleep on a chair in the living room with every light burning in the house would naturally lead one to deduce that you are afraid of placing yourself in the vulnerable position of being in a bed in a dark house."

All the fight went out of Megan, and her rigidly held shoulders slumped in defeat. "Okay," she admitted tiredly. "I was afraid to go to bed." She looked past him, as if seeing the night beyond the closed front door. "It's pitch-black, and I don't know who might be skulking about out there."

"But I *do* know," he said. "There isn't a soul skulking about out there."

"How do you know?" Megan asked, without pausing to think or reflect.

"I looked." His lips tilted into a chiding smile. "I peeked behind every tree and bush."

"I should have known," Megan confessed, giving him an apologetic smile in return. "You are exceptionally thorough in your work, aren't you?"

"Exceptionally," Royce agreed, without so much as a shadow of underlying conceit. "Besides," he went on, shrugging, "I asked the local municipal patrolman to keep a sharp eye on the place while making his sweep of the area."

"Thank you, Royce," Megan said, in quiet recognition of his dedication beyond the call. "I appreciate your concern for my safety."

"Enough to offer me a hot drink?" he asked, arching his burnished brows over eyes beginning to sparkle with inner laughter. "It's cold work beating the bushes and peering behind trees, especially when said bushes and trees are coated with a fine film of ice." His mouth quirked in an invitation for her to share his amusement. "Bites the fingers, you know."

As had happened before, Megan succumbed to his whimsical appeal to her sense of humor. Though her gurgle of laughter was faint, it was genuine, unforced.

"Coffee or tea?" she asked, turning to hang up his jacket in the foyer closet.

"Tea sounds genteel, and more suited to the midnight hour, but I'd prefer coffee," Royce said. "If you don't mind?"

"Whichever," Megan replied, shrugging to show her unconcern and pivoting to lead the way into the kitchen.

She had no sooner crossed the threshold than her glance settled on the half-eaten sandwich and barely touched glass of milk she had left forgotten on the table.

"I'll just clear away my supper things," she muttered, crossing the room and sweeping the plate and the glass from the table. "Then I'll start the coffee."

"That was your supper?"

Megan winced at the note of censure in Royce's voice. "I wasn't very hungry," she said defensively, moving to the sink. Dumping the milk and the remains of the sandwich, she rinsed the plate and glass, then turned to the coffeemaker.

"Besides nourishment, you need to feed your nerves, Megan," Royce said, sauntering across the room to stand beside her. "Or else you're going to come unglued."

A retort telling him to mind his own business sprang to her lips, but Megan held it in check, recalling the emptiness she had experienced on rising from her stool at the worktable, the weakness of needing to hear her mother's voice, the panic that had gripped her at the jarring ring of the doorbell.

"You're right, I know," she admitted, carefully spooning coffee grounds into the lined basket. "But I never fuss with meals to begin with, and tonight... well..."

"You were more than usually alone?"

"Yes," she said in a grateful murmur, no longer surprised by the depths of his understanding and insight.

"Well, you're no longer alone," Royce said, plucking the water-filled glass pot from her trembling fingers and tipping it over the grate on top of the coffeemaker. "And I'm always hungry." He angled his head to grin at her. "What do you say—should we raid the refrigerator?"

"I'm afraid there's not much to raid. I was planning on doing my grocery shopping on..." Megan's voice faded. She swallowed, then went on gamely, "Saturday morning."

"How about in here?" Royce asked, going to the end wall cabinet. "Any canned goodies, soup and such?"

"Sure," Megan answered, giving him permission to look with a wave of her hand. "Help yourself."

In the end, what Royce helped himself to was a can of luncheon meat, which he sliced and fried in one pan, six eggs, which he beat and scrambled up in another pan, and four pieces of slightly stale bread, which he put Megan in charge of toasting and buttering.

Megan surprised herself by polishing off two pieces of the meat, a quarter portion of the egg mixture, and a slice of toast, liberally buttered and slathered with strawberry preserves. But she passed on the coffee, sipping a small glass of orange juice instead.

The bits of conversation they exchanged during their meal were general and innocuous, light-years removed from the root cause of their association. After they finished eating and clearing the table, and as if they had known each other for years, Royce jotted down items on a scrap of notepaper, Megan calling out to him as she took stock of the end cabinet and the refrigerator, deciding what she needed to pick up at the supermarket.

It was nearing two-thirty in the morning by the time Royce made his way to the front door. Reluctant to see him go, Megan retrieved his jacket from the hall closet and watched, sad-eyed, as he shrugged into it.

"You're okay now?" Royce asked, settling his hat low on his forehead before reaching for the door-knob.

"Yes." Megan dredged up a smile for him. "I feel much better, thank you."

"No thanks necessary, unless it's from me."

Megan frowned. "For what?"

"For our late-night indulgence, or whatever you might call it—a late supper, an early breakfast...." He grinned.

Megan experienced an unfamiliar, unwanted, but definite spark of response of a sensual nature. Dismissing it as absurd, under the circumstances, she returned his grin with a faint, remote and cool smile.

Royce looked baffled for an instant. Then, with a barely discernible shrug, he turned the doorknob and swung open the door. A blast of frigid air swept into the foyer.

"Whoa!" he muttered, stepping outside. "It's cold as a witch's..." He caught himself up short, shrugged again, then went on. "It's damn cold out here." He took another step, wobbled, then straightened. "Like a sheet of glass, too."

"Be careful," Megan called, hovering behind the protection afforded by the door. "And drive carefully."

"I will," Royce promised. "Go inside and shut the door," he ordered. "I want to hear that lock click into place."

"But..."

"Go, Megan, I'm freezing!"

"All right," she snapped, stepping around the door to glare at him. "But call me when you get home," she tacked on.

"Me-gan," Royce groaned. "I'll be all right."

"I want to know you aren't wrapped around a tree somewhere," she insisted. "Will you call?"

"Okay, okay, I'll call." He heaved a sigh. "Now, will you get the hell inside?"

"I'm going," she grumbled, moving back behind the door. "Good night, Sergeant."

"Good night, Megan," Royce responded in a tone of rapidly dwindling patience. "Lock the door."

"Sorehead!" Megan shut the door with a bang, then bullied the lock into place.

Royce's bark of laughter reached her, even filtered through the wood-encased steel door.

As had happened before—was it once, twice?—Megan could not deny the chuckle that escaped through her smiling lips. And it was the tug on her lips, the very sound of her soft laughter, that brought home to her the realization of how beneficial his unexpected visit had been to her.

By his very presence, his easy manner, his everything-under-control attitude, Royce had effectively chased the fears, real and imagined, from her rattled mind.

Decent? Megan mused, absently drifting from room to room, extinguishing lights as she went. Royce Wolfe was a lot more than a decent individual; he was the genuine article, a *man*, in every true sense of the word.

Returning to her bedroom, Megan began undressing. Distracted by her thoughts, she was unconscious of the wide, uncovered windows flanking her desk and worktable, the late-winter darkness beyond the panes.

Stripped to the buff, she gathered up her discarded clothing, grabbed a clean oversize navy-blue nightshirt emblazoned with white lettering spelling out Penn State Nitney Lions, and made for the bathroom and a quick, hot shower.

Still contemplating the man who had so recently departed for his own place, and whose call she was expecting momentarily, Megan reentered the bedroom, clad in the nightshirt and a liberal application of face and body lotion.

What facets did he possess that, to her way of thinking, made Royce the living, breathing embodiment of her personal ideal of what a man should be?

Megan mulled over the question as she plied a brush to her shower dampened, tangled mass of long auburn hair.

Appealing surface attractions aside—great bone structure, riveting crystal-blue eyes, a mouth both firm and sensuous, set in a well-shaped head crowned by a vibrant shock of sun-tipped golden brown hair and sitting atop a tall, muscularly trim, fantastic body—Royce Wolfe possessed inner qualities that, in her opinion, surpassed mere appearance, however handsome and sexy-looking he was.

In the short time Megan had known him—had it really only been two days?—Royce had displayed to her a wide and deep range of personality traits.

While Royce was blatantly male, strong, self-confident, determined, even a tad arrogant, he was also understanding, concerned, caring and sensitive... to the point that he had opted for a desk job when the growing routine slaughter of the highway scene, the investigations into cases involving robbery, rape, murder and mayhem had gotten to him.

The very fact that Royce had not only identified and faced his occupational dilemma, but acted to remove himself from the crux of the problem, while maintaining a position within the profession he so obviously loved, told Megan a lot about the man, as a man.

A sobering thought struck. Megan's hand stilled, the brush midway along a silky strand of red hair. The very fact that she was mentally evaluating the man told Megan a lot about her own feelings.

She was interested in the man.

Interested? a taunting inner voice chided.

Try intrigued.

Try excited.

Try...

All right! Megan thought, silencing the inner voice with the acknowledgment.

Royce interests, intrigues and excites me, but—

The phone rang.

Royce!

Dropping the brush to the dressertop, Megan ran for the console on the corner of the desk. She snatched up the receiver in the middle of the second ring.

"Hello?"

Silence.

Megan frowned. Definitely not Royce. But then who? A chill crawled along her spine.

"Hello, who's calling?" she demanded, despairing at the note of incipient panic she heard in her voice.

Nothing.

A large, hulking image filled her mind, terrorizing her senses, stealing her common sense. Reacting to instinct, Megan slammed down the receiver, then stood frozen, staring at the instrument, as if afraid it would leap from the cradle and lunge for her constricted throat.

It rang again.

Oh, my god, oh, my god, oh, my god! A low, keening wail broke from Megan's throat. No. No. Please, no.

A second ring, and then a third.

Not breathing, afraid to think, Megan extended a shaking hand and grabbed the receiver.

"Who is this?" she cried. "Why are you doing this to—"

"What the hell?" Royce exclaimed into her ear. "Megan! What's going on?"

"Oh, Royce! Oh, Royce!" Megan's voice was little more than a sobbing gasp. "I...I just had a phone call...but nobody spoke. It was him. I know it was *him!*"

"Megan, listen to me," Royce commanded her in a calm, stern tone of voice. "Don't fly apart. I'm on my way. I'll be there in a few minutes. Keep it together, honey. I'm coming."

He disconnected. The dial tone buzzed in Megan's ear. Gripping the receiver, she stood, repeating his promise over and over to herself.

I'm on my way. I'll be there in a few minutes. Keep it together, honey. I'm coming.

Honey?

A chill of a different nature scurried down Megan's spine. Surely it had been nothing more than a spur-of-the-moment expression. Royce certainly hadn't meant it as an endearment—had he?

Megan swallowed, and felt a spark of something in her stomach.

Honey?

The beeping noise from the phone penetrated the speculative thoughts distracting her mind.

"If you want to make a call—" the tinny voice of the recording grated against her ears, and patience, "—hang up and dial again."

"Take a flying leap," Megan muttered, sighing in relief when the instrument went silent.

Clutching the now-dead receiver to her chest, Megan kept it together as best she could until, at last, after what seemed like hours, but in actuality couldn't have been more than ten minutes, she heard the blessed sound of crunching tires and squealing brakes from Royce's car in the driveway.

The telephone receiver landed on the carpeted floor with a dull thud. Megan didn't hear it—she was already dashing from the room to the foyer and the front door.

"Megan!" Royce yelled, rapping his knuckles hard against the door. "Are you all right?"

Unaware that she was sobbing, Megan fumbled with the lock with trembling fingers. Cursing, she finally released the lock, pulled the door open, and literally flung her shaking body against the reassuringly solid wall of Royce's chest.

Six

Royce's arms automatically closed around Megan's shivering body. Holding her tightly to him, he stepped into the foyer and nudged the door shut with a backward tap of his heel.

She was even taller than he had first decided; her nuzzling face fit neatly into the curve of his neck.

The broken sound of her uneven, hiccuping breaths impelled him to tighten his arms protectively, drawing her pliant form more closely to his alert-tautened body.

Royce immediately knew he had made a mistake. The feel of Megan's soft curves pressed against him caused an instantaneous reactive response.

He was at once hard and hurting.

Fortunately, Megan appeared to be too upset to notice the pressure against her abdomen.

Silently cursing the inconvenient and inappropriate, if normal and natural, reaction of his flesh and senses, Royce exerted iron-willed control over his gathering response and murmured words of comfort and reassurance.

"It's all right, Megan. I'm here," he said, loosening his arms to clasp her shoulders and move her back a step, away from physical contact with him. "I'm not going to let anything or anybody hurt you."

"But... but suppose it was *him?*" Megan cried, raising a hand to swipe at her wet cheeks. "That...that hulking, horrible man?" she went on, voice rising.

"Calm down, calm down," Royce said in a soothing voice, flexing his fingers gently in her soft flesh, attempting to instill his strength in her. "You told me you had never seen the man before, and that he hadn't called you by your name. Didn't you?"

Megan gulped and nodded. "Yes."

"Well then, I'd say that chances are it was a wrong number, probably dialed by a person with an unsteady finger, or someone who raised one glass too many."

"Do you honestly think so?" she asked, in a small voice so filled with hope it tore at his heart.

"Yes, I do." Royce infused adamant conviction into his voice. "It happens." He shrugged. "It's happened to me. Sometimes you hear a slurred voice, demanding to speak to someone you've never heard of, but more often the offender just hangs up, like the inconsiderate drunk he probably is."

"Yes." Megan gave a quick nod. "I've had a few calls like that at my place in New York."

Royce could see her fighting to suppress the panic that had threatened to overtake her. He could also see the enticing peaks of her breasts, and the sweet curves of her hips and tush, barely concealed by the soft cotton nightshirt. Beneath the midthigh hem of the shirt, her long, shapely legs were exposed for his joyful examination.

Royce dragged his gaze away from her body, back to her pale cheeks and fright-widened eyes. Megan looked exhausted, in need of a lot of hours of solid sleep. Dark shadows pooled in the hollows under her eyes. Weariness tugged her tempting lips into a drooping curve.

He smothered a sigh, and managed a smile.

"Why don't you go to bed?"

"Bed?" Megan's eyes grew wider still, and she shook her head rapidly back and forth. "No. I can't... No!"

"Megan, honey, c'mon," Royce said, smoothing his palms down her arms. "I'll give the area a good once-over, make sure there are no intruders lurking about, before I leave."

"Leave!" Megan yelped, bringing her hands up to grasp his shirt and inadvertently digging her nails into his chest. "You're going to leave? You can't leave! What if the phone rings again?" Though she had asked, she didn't wait for an answer, but rattled on, "I couldn't sleep, not now, not if you leave. I just know I'd sit staring at the phone until morning."

Feeling the stab of her nails in his skin, all the way down to the burgeoning heat of his desire, Royce heaved another, deeper sigh.

"Okay, okay...." He surrendered, purely in self-defense. "I'll stay, but—"

"Oh, Royce, thank you." Megan eased her nails from his skin to smooth her palms over the front of his shirt—unconsciously, he felt sure. "I know it's a dreadful imposition, but I'll sit up with you. Uh, are you hungry, thirsty? I can..."

"No, we just ate, remember?" he said, interrupting her. "And you will not sit up with me. *You're* going to bed." Letting his hands fall away from the allure of her soft arms, he motioned toward the darkened living room. "I'll stretch out on the recliner in there."

A frown tugged at Megan's brow as she shifted her gaze from him to the recliner, then back to him, sweeping a glance down the length of his body.

"You can't rest in that chair," she protested. "It's not nearly big enough for you."

Since she wasn't telling him anything he didn't already know, Royce merely shrugged. "What would you suggest?" he asked, rather dryly. "The sofa?"

"Uh, no...." Megan shook her head. "If anything, the sofa's even smaller than the chair."

"Right." Royce nodded. "So?"

"There's the guest room." Megan indicated the second door along the hallway with a flick of her hand.

"I don't think so." Royce shook his head. "I don't want to get too comfortable."

She bit her lip, and gave him a helpless look.

"Uh-huh." Royce returned her look with one of his own—not helpless, but knowing. "I'll stretch out on the chair."

"Oh, Royce..." she began, in a low tone of contrition. "I'm sorry, but—"

He cut her off, gently. "Not to worry. I've managed to catch some zees in worse positions." He laughed easily. "Believe it or not, I actually dozed off standing up on a train some years back." His smile grew into a grin at the skeptical look she gave him. "No kidding. Fortunately, I jerked awake when the train pulled in at my station, or, who knows, like that guy in the song, I mighta been the man who never returned."

Megan laughed, and though the sound was weak, Royce considered it a good indicator of her easing tension. Acting on it, he again clasped her arms and turned her around to face her bedroom doorway. Then he gave her a light nudge to get her moving.

"Go, Megan," he ordered. "Get some rest."

"But—" she again began in protest, tossing a concerned look over her shoulder at him.

"No buts. Cut me a break, please. I'm tired, too." He yawned elaborately, if indelicately, to prove his assertion. "Get going."

She sighed, but gave in. "Okay." She took two hesitant steps, then, spinning to face him, insisted, "But I know I won't be able to sleep."

Royce simply smiled at her.

"I mean it."

"All right, just go rest your eyes for a while."

The fight went out of her, yet it was still only with evident reluctance that Megan went into her room. Moments later, she opened the door a crack and thrust her arm out, extending the extra comforter she'd obviously just thought to give him.

"You'll need this," she said, calling him back up the three steps to the hallway. "The house is chilly now."

"Thank you," he murmured, relieving her of the lightweight down cover. "Now go to bed."

"Good night," she whispered, peering around the door at him. "But I still say I won't sleep."

"Well then, you rest, and I'll sleep." Royce offered her a wry smile. "Wake me if you need me, okay?"

"Yes."

Her shadowed eyes brought a tightness to his throat and a pang to his chest. Royce heaved a breath and swallowed in a futile attempt to relieve both. Giving up, he smiled again and turned toward the steps into the living room.

"Good night, honey."

* * *

Honey.

Megan lay curled up in the center of her bed, beneath the down comforter, repeating his casually voiced endearment over and over inside her tired mind.

And deep inside her weary body a flicker of warmth ignited in response to the mental echo.

Honey.

It meant nothing, of course, Megan told herself sleepily, uncertain whether the thought was in connection to the endearment, or the unfurling sensation of warm arousal she felt.

She shifted position to dislodge the feeling; the warmth merely intensified.

Ridiculous, Megan told herself. She was suffering mild trauma and shock. She could not be responding sensually to such an offhand, probably unconscious, endearment.

Could she?

The inner warmth spread, causing a tingling along the inside of her thighs, and at their apex.

Megan shifted position again, only this time her movements were sinuous, languorous. She frowned and moved her head against the pillow in a fruitless bid to deny the proof of her body's sensual response to the physical attraction presented to her by Royce Wolfe.

Royce. The thought of his name created his image; the image drew the tingling sensation from the lower regions of her body to her breasts, her shoulders, her arms, and then to her fingertips. Megan could feel again the solid strength of his flatly muscled chest beneath her fingers, her palms. Her breath grew shallow, her nipples grew taut, the tingling in her thighs grew into a stinging heat of need.

Startled by the sheer intensity of her physical response, Megan coiled her arms around her waist and held on to herself, afraid to move, afraid to think, afraid to face the truth of her own feminine desires.

It simply could not be, Megan told herself. Especially not after what she had so recently endured at the hands of a crude and violent man!

But Royce Wolfe was not a crude and violent man, her exhausted brain reminded her. By his actions, his caring, Royce had revealed himself, his character. She herself had labeled Royce a thoroughly decent man.

Decent.

Nice.

Attractive.

The warm flow inside brought another adjective from Megan's weakening consciousness.

Sexy.

Megan tightened her arms around her slender form, as if instinctively holding herself together.

Honey.

The echo of his voice whispered through her mind, as sweetly as the endearment itself.

But he didn't mean anything by it.

Did he?

Fortunately for Megan, the inner warmth wasn't the only response flowing throughout her body. The languor had crept through her system, to invade her mind, as well. Her eyelids grew heavy. She yawned. Her eyes closed.

Within moments, Megan was drifting, free of the disturbing questions. Lost to the world, she was blithely unaware that not once had she so much as given a thought to the fear of the ringing phone breaking the quiet of the night.

For Royce, ensconced in a chair, his legs and arms dangling from footrests and armrests, it was a very long night. But not only due to the inadequate length of the recliner. His mental discomfort added to his physical unease.

Damned inconvenient time for his libido to go into overdrive, Royce reflected, squirming for the umpteenth time within the close confines of the chair.

Inconvenient, but—considering the circumstances of his recent personal history—not by any means earth-shattering, or even unpredictable, for that matter.

It had been some long months since he had been with a woman...more like a year. Thanks to the crushing effects of being ignominiously dumped by a woman he'd been dangerously close to falling in love with, Royce had spent the previous eleven months cooling his heels, and his libido, so far as the opposite sex was concerned.

But the fact that his celibacy had been self-imposed had little bearing on the current issue. From all indications, his inclination toward abstinence had run its course. Now, thanks to another woman, a tall, willowy redhead, Royce was again back among the ranks of the randy.

Thinking of Megan sent a tongue of fiery desire licking through Royce. He smothered a groan and squirmed again, grunting when his hip made hard contact with the arm of the chair.

Chill out, Wolfe, Royce advised himself disgustedly. Stop acting like a teenager in the throes of a massive hormone explosion, for pity's sa— Royce's thoughts scattered at the sudden sound at the window.

It was the wind, wasn't it? At once wide awake, alert and tense, Royce focused his attention on every slight noise from outside, and slowly, carefully retracted the recliner's footrest and eased his long frame from the chair.

Moving silently on stockinged feet, Royce crossed to the wide window. Hesitating, he listened, straining to hear any sound not produced by nature.

There was only the low moan of the wind, brushing the windows, sighing through the branches of bare limbs and fir trees and small ornamental bushes.

Raising one hand, Royce nudged the edge of the drapery panel aside and peered through the pane. There was only the night, and the pale moonlight glittering on the thin layer of ice sheening the ground.

Damn, would spring never come?

Heaving a sigh, Royce let the drapery panel fall back against its counterpart, then padded into the dining room to inspect the windows there. Nothing. From the dining room, he drifted into the kitchen to repeat the drill, then into the kitchen and the laundry room, and on into the central bathroom. He then went into the remaining two bedrooms, one of which was obviously the master suite used by Megan's parents, the other the guest room Megan had mentioned.

Royce stood for a moment, staring longingly at the single bed. Then, heaving a sigh, he returned to the living room.

Suppressing another sigh, Royce settled once more into the recliner, deciding that, if nothing else, the exercise had been a diversion, an escape from his wayward thoughts about Megan, and his physical response to her allure.

All of which, of course, brought the thoughts and feelings rushing right back.

Damn, Royce groaned in silent misery. It was going to be a *really* long night.

Diffused sunlight filtered between the horizontal mini-blinds brightening the room, waking Megan.

For a moment, she lay still, frowning with the effort of bringing recall to her sleep-fuzzy mind. Then memory kicked in, surging back with a flood of the incidents of the night: the phone call, her near-panic, Royce.

Royce!

Tossing back the comforter, Megan leapt out of bed and, not bothering to take the time to look for her robe, ran to the door, flung it wide, and dashed into the drapery-shrouded living room. At the bottom of the three steps, she came to an abrupt halt, her eyes widening in fascination and admiration.

Royce stood in the center of the room, arms raised over his head, belly sucked in, his long muscles rippling as he stretched the cramps and kinks from his body.

Throwing his head back, he opened his mouth wide in a huge, noisy yawn. That, combined with his pose, and his shock of tawny hair, reminded Megan so much of a big, morning-hungry lion, she couldn't stifle the giggle that burst from her throat.

Lowering and turning his head to face her, Royce gave her a quizzical look. "Something funny?"

"No." Megan clapped a hand over her mouth to smother another giggle, then spread her fingers to continue through them, "I, uh... You just struck me as looking like a big, disgruntled cat, stretching and growling."

"I wasn't growling, I was yawning." Royce silently padded across the room to her. A slow, feral, devastatingly effective smile curved his attractive mouth. "If I growl, honey, you'll know it."

There it was again, the careless endearment, so casually tossed out, so potent in impact.

Megan's breath caught, and she fought against revealing the confusion and mixed emotions she was experiencing. She smiled. It quivered, then stuck to her dry lips.

"Uh, do you growl often?" she asked, for want of something, anything, to say.

His smile grew into a Wolfe-ish grin. "Now and again," he drawled. "At my men, when I'm seriously pi—ah, ticked off." His voice lowered to a near-purr. "And occasionally, but altogether differently, when I'm caught up in the throes of passion."

A bolt of sensation, crackling like heat lightning, shot through Megan. Suddenly, her lips were not only dry, they felt hot. Her breasts felt heavy. Her body felt...empty.

Royce said something; she shook her head. "What?"

His lips twitched. "I asked if you ever growled while in the throes of passion?"

How had she gotten into this discussion? Megan wondered wildly, raking her mind for a coherent reply.

"Uh, no...." Well, she had raked for coherent, not brilliant, or even intelligent.

"Pity," Royce murmured.

"Pity?" Megan frowned. "Why?"

"Oh, just an off-the-wall opinion of mine." His blue eyes were bright, teasing.

She was almost afraid to ask, but of course she had to. "Which is?"

"That unless you've reached the point of growling, you haven't truly plumbed the depths, or tested the fire, of the throes of passion."

Megan couldn't believe she was having this conversation with any man, let alone a man she hardly knew. And she was still in her nightshirt, to boot! She couldn't decide whether she wanted to laugh or run back into her bedroom.

Not the bedroom!

Resisting an impulse to tug at the hem of her nightshirt, she opted to laugh.

Royce laughed with her. "I warned you that my opinion was off-the-wall."

"I'm beginning to think that *you're* off-the-wall," Megan said, only half teasingly. "Or that you think I might be."

"No, I don't think that, honey." Royce's tone was now deadly serious. "I'm beginning to think you're rather special."

Honey. Rather special. Megan felt a distinct melting sensation inside. Fighting the feeling, and the attraction of the man who had caused it, Megan withdrew behind a cool front of composure.

"I think I'd better get dressed," she said, backing away from him.

"I've offended you." Royce's voice revealed both concern and regret. "I'm sorry."

"Offended?" Megan shook her head, and came to an abrupt halt when her bare right heel banged into the bottom step leading down into the living room. "I don't understand. Why would I feel offended?"

"The teasing. I mean, after what you've been through, for one thing." He shrugged. "Then, for another, my calling you honey." He gave a quirky smile. "I know a lot of women object to that these days."

"Uh, no... I, uh, no, I'm not offended," she said, slightly amazed that she was not. In truth, Megan had sometimes taken exception to the occasional male usage of off-hand endearments like *honey* and *sweetie* and—shudder—*babe*. And yet, when the endearment came from Royce, she felt... flattered.

Strange. But, stranger still, in light of her recent terrifying experience, was the somewhat shocking realization that she wasn't put off by his teasing, but was in fact actually enjoying it!

"I'm glad," Royce said, his expression revealing his evident relief. "Because I meant no offense."

"I know." The really funny part was, Megan did know. It was all much too strange, and so made her feel awkward, uncertain, and as giddy as a teenager in the first flush of her first real crush.

Definitely time to get dressed, she scolded herself, again absently tugging on the hem of her nightshirt.

"Ah, if you'll give me a few moments," she babbled, sliding her heel up the riser to the bottom step, "I'll dash into my room and throw on some clothes, then make you breakfast."

"That's not necessary," Royce said, unconvincingly, turning away to lift the comforter from the chair and begin folding it. "I can grab something to eat on my way home."

"You certainly will not," Megan said indignantly. "Making you breakfast is the least I can do to repay you for your trouble." An impish grin played over her lips. "Most especially the discomfort you endured in that chair." Not giving him a chance to respond, she whirled around, took the top two steps in one long stride, and went running to her room.

His soft laughter ran after her.

Seven

Breakfast was an unqualified success. The French toast was a perfect golden brown, the small sausage links were tangy, not too spicy, the coffee was rich and delicious.

Cradling his refilled mug in his hands, Royce sat back in his chair, stretched his legs out and smiled his utter satisfaction at his hostess.

"That was great," he told her. "You're really a very good cook. I feel almost human now."

"Thank you." A becoming flush of pleasure tinged Megan's cheeks. "Almost human?"

"Hmm..." Royce nodded and took a tentative sip of the still-steaming brew. Washed by last night's misty rainfall, the morning had dawned sparkling. The sunlight streaming through the windows shot gleaming red highlights through the long, loose strands of Megan's hair and enhanced the color pinkening her cheeks. Quashing an impulse to reach across the table and stroke the spiral curls, and her soft skin, Royce explained, "I'll feel a lot more human after I've caught a few hours' sleep."

"Oh, Royce, I'm sorry." Megan looked both downcast and embarrassed. "I'm such a wuss."

"Bag that, honey," he ordered, gently. "Your reaction to that phone call was perfectly normal," he assured her. "Whatever the hell normal is."

The shadows lifted from her eyes. A tiny smile kissed her full, luscious lips. Royce envied the smile.

"You don't know what normal is?" she asked, raising one naturally arched auburn eyebrow chidingly.

"No," he admitted easily. "I used to think I knew, but—" he shrugged "—the longer I live, the more I realize how little I do know." His expression grew wry. "Hell, I used to think I knew most of the answers. Now the only thing I really know is that I don't even know half the questions."

Megan laughed—which, of course, was the response he had worked for. She was so damned appealing when she laughed. Come to that, she was damned appealing when she didn't laugh. Like earlier this morning, he reflected, sensation stirring at the memory of Megan, her enticing form barely covered by that oversize nightshirt.

Not that she wasn't alluring in the soft jeans and baggy sweatshirt she had "thrown on" after beating her hasty retreat into the bedroom, Royce allowed, surreptitiously caressing the outline of the breasts concealed beneath the shirt. But, oh, her long, long legs... Megan's legs were the stuff of his wildest erotic fantasies.

Smothering a yearning sigh, and a leap of life in the lower section of his body, Royce took another sip of coffee... in reality, a big gulp.

"It is rather ironic, isn't it?" she said, her tone as wry as his expression. She was apparently innocently oblivious of his lascivious mental meanderings. "The older we grow, the less we know. Kinda like that old Pennsylvania Dutch saying—The faster I go, the behinder I get."

"Yeah." Royce chuckled, finished off his coffee in two long swallows, then, drawing back his legs, jack-knifed to his feet. "I'm headed for home and bed." He leveled a questioning look at her. "You'll be all right now, on your own?"

"Yes, thank you." Megan gave him a bright and brave smile. "At the risk of sounding trite, I suppose things always do look brighter in the light of day, don't they?" She returned his questioning look.

"Trite, maybe, but true," Royce agreed, bending over the table to collect his plate, cup and utensils.

"No!" Megan ordered, reaching across the table to place a staying hand over his. "I'll do that."

"You cooked," he reminded her unnecessarily, feeling his skin begin to prickle and grow warm beneath her palm. "I don't mind clearing up."

"I appreciate the thought," Megan said, flexing her hand over his in a reassuring squeeze. "But you've done enough. Go home, Royce. Get some sleep. You have to work tonight."

"Yeah." Royce nodded, and stifled a yawn, along with a responsive groan at her touch. "Okay, I'm outa here." He straightened, dislodging her hand from atop his. His flesh immediately felt cooler, robbed of warmth. "Is my jacket in the foyer closet?"

"Uh, yes!" Unfastening her gaze from her now-empty hand, Megan jerked around and made a beeline for the hallway. "I'll get it for you."

Sauntering after her, Royce pondered the significance of the fleeting, almost bereft, expression that had flickered over Megan's face as she stared at her empty hand. A curl of hopeful excitement unwound inside him. Could it be possible? he wondered, catching his breath as the excitement ribboned along his nervous system. Could Megan possibly be feeling as strong an attraction to him as he felt for her?

Heady stuff, thoughts like that, Royce told himself, feeling suddenly revived, alert, not at all sleepy. His eyes sought hers as he came to a halt. Megan met his questioning stare for an instant, then lowered her eyes and thrust her hand forward, nearly tossing his jacket at him.

Without taking his contemplative gaze off her, Royce caught the garment and shucked into it. Why couldn't she look at him? he mused, absently fastening the jacket. The curl of excitement inside him flared into full-blown desire when the only reasonable answer sprang to mind.

Megan *was* attracted to him, maybe even strongly attracted to him. A thrill skittered down Royce's spine; hope sprouted in his mind like a spring blossom.

Him and Megan. Together.

An image rose in his imagination, complete in every sensuous, body-tormenting detail, of him and Megan, naked, entwined, together. Maybe. Someday.

Royce's chest muscles contracted, cutting off his breath. His arms ached with the longing to hold her. His palms burned with the need to touch, caress, every inch of her. His mouth tingled with the yearning to kiss her. The rest of his hurting body didn't bear thinking about.

Royce moved to go to her. Then he caught himself up short, pivoted and strode to the door.

Dammit, Wolfe, Royce railed at himself. *Stop reacting like a libido-driven idiot. The absolute last thing Megan needs right now is more emotional trauma.*

Get out. Go home. And grow up.

"Thanks again for breakfast," he said, hating the dry, strangled sound of his own voice.

"Thanks again for staying," Megan replied, sounding almost as strained and affected as he felt.

His fingers fumbled with the dead bolt and the safety lock. Damn. He hadn't fumbled with anything, or anyone, since his fourteenth summer. "Glad to be of service," he muttered, sighing in relief when, at last, the door swung open.

"Will you..." Megan's voice faded on an uncertain note, forcing him to glance around at her.

The shadows of confusion and doubt in her blue eyes tore a hole in his gut. Royce wanted nothing so much at that moment as to pull Megan into his arms, cradle her protectively against his hard body.

Make love to her.

Run for it, Wolfe, before you run to her.

"What?" he asked, sidling through the doorway.

"It's mild!"

"Huh?" Royce blinked.

"The day. The weather." Megan gave him a helpless look. "It's mild outside."

"Oh." Now who was confused? Royce thought, knowing the answer. Collecting himself, he stepped outside to test the air temperature. Damned if it *wasn't* mild, springlike. "Yeah," he said. "Feels good."

"Too good to stay indoors."

Royce frowned. "You're planning on going somewhere?"

"I need to do some grocery shopping," Megan said, reminding him of her empty refrigerator. "Why?"

"You have no wheels," Royce answered, in turn reminding her of her wrecked car. "You're welcome to use my car," he offered. "You could drop me—"

Megan silenced him with a quick shake of her head. The sunlight caught and tangled in her hair again, seemingly turning it into a fiery mass framing her face.

Royce curled his fingers into his palm to keep from reaching out to entangle them in the flamelike strands.

"... in the garage," she was saying.

"I beg your pardon," he admitted apologetically, "but I missed the first part of what you said." Idiot!

"I said—" Megan spoke distinctly "—thank you, but that's not necessary. My father's car is in the garage. He asked me to drive it every so often, anyway."

"Yeah, it's not good to let it sit." Royce frowned. "What had you started to say before?"

She mirrored his frown. "Before when?"

"You said 'will you...' and then stopped." He lifted one eyebrow. "Will I what?"

Megan looked uncomfortable, embarrassed. She flicked a glance at him, then immediately glanced away again. She wet her lips, cleared her throat, then shook her head. "It was nothing. I, uh, never mind...."

"C'mon, Meg," Royce said on a long sigh. "It must have been something. And you should know by now that you can ask me anything. What is it?"

Still she hesitated, her soft mouth twisting in a self-mocking grimace. "I, uh, can I?"

"Can you what?" he asked, thoroughly confused.

"Ask you anything."

"Didn't I just say you could?" Royce was experiencing a distinct sensation of going around in circles. "Ask."

Megan drew a breath, and began slowly, "I was just wondering...well..." She paused, the went on in a rush. "I was wondering if you were thinking of stopping by tonight, you know, when you're done working?"

Royce felt hard-pressed to keep from laughing. "You had to work up your courage to ask that?" he said, losing the battle to hold back a teasing smile.

"Well..." She shrugged. "I have no right to ask you to look out for me in your free time."

"But you didn't ask," he pointed out. "Not initially. It was my idea to stop by last night, remember?"

"Yes, but—"

"So," he said, blithely interrupting her, "I'll stop by. I was planning to, anyway." His teasing smile grew up, into a grin. "Were you thinking about offering me a reward for dedication to duty above and beyond the call?"

"Reward?" Megan frowned. "What sort of reward?"

On the spot, Royce decided that Megan was the only woman he knew who looked appealing when she frowned. But then, he decided, she looked appealing most of the time. Too appealing for his peace of mind. A response to her appeal stirred, in his emotions, in his body.

That was when he decided he had better stick to the discussion at hand. "Well, since I usually have a snack when I get home from work," he said, "a cup of decaf coffee or hot chocolate and a couple of sandwiches would be nice."

"A couple of sandwiches!" Megan exclaimed on a choking bout of the giggles. "At that time of night?"

"Hey, honey, give me a break, will ya?" Royce groused, in patently false aggrievement, deciding her giggle was appealing, as well, and that he had really better get going...and soon. "Look at me." He swept his arm down to indicate his tall form. "I'm a big man. How far do you think one small sandwich will go in filling me up?"

"I see your point," Megan conceded solemnly, her gleaming blue eyes belying her somber tone. "I will be happy to prepare a snack for you."

"You've got yourself a deal," Royce said. "I'll—" He broke off, just then noticing the shivering tremor in her body. He cursed himself for not noticing sooner. "You're cold. It's not quite spring yet. Go inside. I'm going home to bed." He started for his car, but called back to her over his shoulder, "By the way, I like most kinds of luncheon meats, but most especially baked ham with cheese."

"You'll have it, Sergeant," Megan promised. "Whatever turns you on."

Laughing, Royce gave her a quick wave, slid behind the wheel, fired the engine and backed out of the driveway. His laughter ceased abruptly as soon as he was out of her sight.

You'll have it, Sergeant. Megan's promise replayed in his mind. *Whatever turns you on.*

Not hardly, Royce thought, reflexively tightening his grip on the wheel. He liked ham-and-cheese sandwiches, but they did not turn him on.

Megan turned him on.

His libido was at full throttle and humming along at way above the legal speed limit.

Royce wanted Megan so bad, so very much, it shocked him. The very intensity of his desire for her was startling, for he had never before in his life felt anything quite like it, not even during his supposedly most potent, late-teen years.

Royce made it home safely to his bachelor apartment, driving by rote, with automatic expertise. He had had no doubts about making it home safely.

But being able to get to sleep while his imagination created explicit fantasies around Megan—that he *did* have serious doubts about.

His doubts proved well-founded.

Royce tossed and turned, grunted and groaned, and didn't sleep worth a damn.

But he did enjoy the fantasies.

Megan had a wonderful time grocery shopping. In no hurry, she wandered up and down the aisles, perusing the items on the shelves, making both careful and impulsive selections.

Which just went to highlight how long it had been since she had shopped for food for anybody other than herself, she mused, frowning indecisively at the price on a packaged thick-cut Delmonico steak.

Deciding Royce deserved the expense, she tossed the package into her already piled-high basket and pushed it farther along the meat section.

Four tiny lamb chops followed the steak into the cart; they were for her. Remembering that Royce liked ham, she added a breakfast ham steak to the growing mound.

Megan didn't so much as blink at the cost of feeding Royce, but merely smiled benignly at the pleasant clerk as she handed over the stack of bills.

Considering all he had done, and planned to continue doing, in addition to his caring, gentle concern for her, Megan figured the least she could do was provide not just adequate but delicious sustenance for him.

Besides, she had discovered that morning that she enjoyed cooking for a man. Well, not simply a man, or any man, Megan qualified, grunting as she bullied the stuffed shopping bags out of the cart and into the trunk of her father's car.

She enjoyed cooking for Royce.

What did that tell her?

The question caught Megan unawares as she settled into the driver's seat and pulled the door shut after her. Her expression pensive, she examined the question. The exercise did not overtax her capabilities, even though the answer that presented itself did surprise her somewhat, in light of the fact that she had known him only a few days.

Megan admitted that she enjoyed cooking for Royce because she liked him.

Liked?

Okay, she conceded to the inner prod. She more than liked him; she felt a strong attraction to him…an emotional, as well as physical, attraction.

But how could that be? After what she had been through a few nights ago, how could she even contemplate the attractions of any man, regardless of how nice he might be?

Biting her lower lip in consternation, Megan switched on the engine and drove off the parking lot. The jarring sound of a blast from the horn of an oncoming car shattered her mental distraction.

Geez! Megan thought, shuddering in reaction. She had missed plowing into that other car by mere inches! The very idea of wrecking her father's car, so soon after totaling her own—not to mention the possible damage she could have inflicted on her own, more vulnerable person—was enough to jerk her into giving her full, undivided attention to her driving.

But a genuine concern about damaging her father's car, a rather expensive top-of-the-line that her father took great pride in, simmered at the edges of Megan's mind as she carefully tooled toward home.

And it was that concern that impelled Megan to impulsively pull onto the lot of a new-and-used-car dealership located along the highway just outside of Conifer.

The car behind her, a beat-up piece of junk with a bad muffler, sped past as she made the turn onto the lot. Megan automatically glanced at the driver, and for an instant, an eerie, uneasy sensation flickered in her mind. There was something about the look of the dark-haired man hunched over the steering wheel.

But the sensation was fleeting, overshadowed by the image of a racy red sports car in the forefront of her mind. Shrugging off the feeling, Megan brought the car to a stop near the entrance to the showroom.

Although the day was mild, Megan knew it certainly wasn't warm enough to affect the meats and frozen foods she had stashed in the trunk—at least not for the short amount of time needed for her to inquire if the dealer had in stock a car the exact style and color of the one she had totaled.

The dealer didn't, to his expressed dismay. But, while he offered to order one from the factory for her, he also was quick to point out the attractions of the wide range of sports styles and colors available and on display, there in the showroom and outside on the lot.

Feeling vaguely as if by merely driving onto the lot she had committed herself to at least looking, Megan allowed the man to escort her around. And, to her surprise, she did find herself admiring another model, in a sleek silver-gray.

Still, undecided, she gave the salesman a bright smile, and a tentative promise.

"I'll, ah, think about it," she said, heading back to her father's car. "I'll come back later in the week," she went on, deciding to ask Royce to accompany her and give her his opinion of the vehicle.

Luckily, the salesman refrained from pressuring her, and simply offered her his card, along with a request that she see him when she returned.

Fair enough, Megan figured as she drove off the lot and into the sparse midday traffic. Telling herself that she had better finish her current project, since she would definitely need the money to put toward whatever car she eventually bought, she sedately drove home.

Megan really didn't breathe easy until after she had unloaded the groceries and shut the garage door, closing her father's car safely inside. Then, after stowing away the foodstuffs, she went to her worktable.

Lost in the advertising layout, Megan was unaware of the passage of time. It was only when long rays of sunlight slanted through the wide windows that she became aware of the waning day, and the emptiness of her stomach.

Standing, she stretched the cramps from her shoulder and back muscles, experiencing a feeling of deep satisfaction as she studied the work in progress.

It was almost finished. And it was good. Megan allowed herself a self-satisfied smile. It was more than good, she thought, congratulating herself.

So there.

Laughing to and at herself, she left the room and went to the kitchen to rustle up supper for one. The prospect held little appeal, but she had to eat.

Meeting Royce, sharing a couple of meals with him, had changed her perspective on dining alone. For some reason, food seemed to look and taste better when Royce was seated opposite her at the table.

Thinking about Royce brought him near; it was almost as if Megan could sense him close by. A thrill tingled along her spine, igniting sparks of warmth throughout her body.

She liked him.

No, Megan told herself, absently eating the ravioli she didn't even remember heating and dishing out for herself. What she was feeling toward Royce had progressed way beyond liking. It was scary, but it was even more exciting.

She glanced at the clock and felt her pulse rate increase; only five or so hours, and Royce would be there. In a futile attempt to bring a measure of order to her errant pulse, and bring herself down to earth, Megan collected her thoughts and made a mental note to ask him about going with her sometime to look at that silver-gray sports car.

With her hunger appeased, and feeling a pleasant afterglow instilled by the satisfaction of a good day's work accomplished, Megan hummed while she washed her few dishes and straightened the kitchen.

The phone rang just as she was centering a bowl of fruit on the table.

Going stiff with reawakened fear, Megan stared at the instrument mounted on the kitchen wall. Barely breathing, she listened as it rang, twice, three times, four times. Then, impatience flaring at her own trepidation, she stormed across the room and snatched up the receiver.

"Hello?" she snapped in a sharp-edged, somewhat threatening tone of voice.

"Megan?"

Relief washed through her at the puzzled sound of Jefferson Clarke's voice. "Oh, Jeff, it's you!" Megan replied, giving a light burst of relieved laughter.

"Yes," he said, still sounding puzzled. "Were you expecting a call from someone else?"

"No!" she said, too quickly.

"Megan, you sound strange. Is something wrong?"

For one brief moment, Megan was tempted to pour out her tale of woe to Jeff, but then the moment passed, and she shook her head, denying herself the self-indulgence. What purpose would be served by her dumping her troubles on Jeff, when he was in New York and she was in Pennsylvania?

Besides, Royce's shoulders were broader than Jeff's.

Rolling her eyes at the unfairness of the comparison, even though it was valid, Megan hastened to reassure him.

"Not a thing," she prevaricated. "I was, uh, preoccupied, and the ringing phone startled me."

"I see," he murmured. "I think."

"Are you calling to harass me about being late with the layout?" she asked, changing the subject.

"You are over deadline," Jeff reminded her gently. "But that isn't the only reason I called. I was concerned when you didn't return my call. That isn't like you."

"Uh, well, I'm sorry, but..." A low buzz sounded, indicating that there was another call waiting. "I've been busy," Megan went on, ignoring the buzz. "But I have good news. I'm almost finished with the—" The buzz sounded again.

"Perhaps you had better answer that," Jeff suggested, obviously annoyed by the interruption.

"Okay, hang on," Megan said, sighing, as she depressed the disconnect button.

"Hello?"

Nothing.

"Hello?" Megan repeated, thinking only that Jeff was waiting, very likely with mounting impatience.

Again there was silence.

Sighing once more, Megan punched the disconnect button. "Jeff, are you still there?"

"Yes, I'm here," he answered, testily. "Was it someone important?"

"No. As a matter of fact, whoever it was got impatient and hung up," she told him, silently praying that it hadn't been Royce trying to reach her. "Now, where were we?"

"You were telling me you were almost finished with the layout."

"Yes!" she said happily. "I expect to finish tomorrow and put it in the mail to you the day after."

"I have a better idea," he said softly.

"Really?" Megan frowned. "What's that?"

"Why don't you bring it over?" he asked. "We could see a show, have a late dinner, talk over drinks."

And go round and round again about deepening their relationship, having an affair, Megan thought, filling in the blanks he'd left unspoken.

"Oh, I don't know, Jeff," she began, even though she did. But there was no way she'd consider anything other than platonic friendship with him now, after meeting Royce.

"Will you at least think about it?"

There was a note of abject pleading in his tone that was so totally out of character for the usually ultraurbane Jeff that Megan didn't have the heart to respond with a flat no.

"Yes, I'll think about it." Though she'd reluctantly agreed, Megan felt it was only fair to add a qualifying warning. "But please don't build up any expectations, Jeff."

"We'll see," he murmured. "It's enough for me to know that you'll think about it."

"I will."

And Megan did think about it, for all of ten seconds after they said their goodbyes.

After that, she only had thoughts for Royce, thoughts of concern that the call waiting had been from him trying to reach her to tell her that he wouldn't be stopping by after all.

For Megan, the following hours seemed like days, which indicated a great deal more than she was ready to face about her growing feelings for Royce Wolfe.

But she did derive one benefit from the long wait. In a bid to fill the dragging hours, Megan went back to work.

The project was finished!

Eight

Royce slowed the car to make the turn into Megan's driveway, and cast a quick glance in the rearview mirror at the vehicle that had been following behind him ever since he turned off the interstate some miles back.

At any other time, the presence of the car probably wouldn't even have caught his attention, but at 12:05 in the morning it was unusual.

Though Royce occasionally passed a car, or, more often, a truck, on the interstate on his way home from work, as a rule he seldom did once he had entered the limits of the town, which for all intents and purposes rolled up its sidewalks along about 10:00 p.m. or so.

The car following Royce—a beat-up junker, from what he could see of it—also slowed down, then, with a rumble from the muffler, speeded up again.

Someone lost on the side road? Royce mused, toying with the idea of backing out of the drive and trailing the vehicle. Or someone interested in a particular driveway leading to the home of a certain woman?

The question bothered Royce, for three reasons. The first was the information he had received earlier that evening from the municipal patrolman, concerning a couple of calls to the station from residents in this area, reporting complaints about an unfamiliar car with a noisy muffler, cruising the area with apparent aimlessness.

The second reason it bothered Royce was the very fact that Megan was alone in a house set in the very center of the area from which those complaints had come.

The third, but by no means the least, of those reasons was the persistent memory of the phone call Megan had received late last night. For all his downplaying of the importance of that call to her, Royce had a nagging, uneasy suspicion that the call had not been the result of some drunk's inability to punch in the correct numbers. Instinct, or intuition, or *something,* made him feel certain the call had been placed deliberately by Megan's attacker.

Or was he simply getting slightly paranoid due to his increasing personal interest in Megan?

But the car did have a noisy muffler.

That thought settled the issue for Royce. His personal interest aside, he was first and foremost a law officer. Throwing the car into reverse, he backed out of the driveway and shot down the road after the vehicle.

Fifteen frustrating minutes later, Royce pulled into the driveway again. His pursuit had proved fruitless; he hadn't been able to find sight or sound of the car.

Knowing the driver of the car could have sought cover in any number of places in that secluded, heavily wooded area exacerbated the tension and sense of unease mounting in Royce with regard to Megan's safety.

If anything happened to her...

Clamping a lid on his thoughts, Royce exited the car and strode to the house.

Nothing was going to happen to Megan, he assured himself. Because he was going to make damn sure nothing happened to her, even if he had to cuff her to his wrist to do so.

That thought, and the image that came with it, brought a wry smile to Royce's lips.

Wolfe, old son, you really have got it bad, he told himself, raising his hand to rap his knuckles against the door. Too bad you can't put the woman in your pocket.

The door opened. Megan stood there, a flowing silk caftan caressing her body, her red mane framing her lovely face, a smile of welcome on her inviting lips.

Better yet, too bad you can't pick her up and put her in your bed, Royce thought, feeling every molecule in his body respond to the sight of her.

"Hello."

Her soft voice shivered through Royce, causing a chill in his spine, and a fire in his loins. Suppressing a groan, he worked his lips into a smile.

"Hello. Everything all right?"

"Yes, everything's fine." Megan stepped back, swinging the door wide. "Come in. It feels like the night air stole the promise of spring from the day."

"Yeah," Royce agreed, following her inside. "But it sure felt good for a change."

"Yes, it felt wonderful." She lowered her gaze to his chest, frowning when all she saw was his shirt. "Where's your jacket?" she asked, then answered for him. "In the car."

"Right." Royce grinned.

Shaking her head in despair, all the while grinning along with him, Megan turned and started down the hallway. "Hungry?" she asked, continuing on, as if certain of his answer.

"Starved," Royce admitted, conceding to her certainty. "I made do with a doughnut for dinner."

"A doughnut!" Megan stopped dead to shoot an appalled look at him. "I thought you were the guy who needed a lot of food to fill up his big body."

Royce laughed. "I am." His lips curled into a blatantly wicked smile. "The doughnut had a rich cream filling."

"Oh, wonderful." Megan rolled her eyes. "Empty calories, fats, all that good stuff."

"I only ate it to stave off the hunger," he explained, losing the fight against another grin. "I wanted to save it for the snack you promised me tonight."

"Then consider yourself lucky that I did go grocery shopping today," she retorted, striding into the kitchen. "I have everything ready," she said as he stepped up to her side. She motioned with her hand, indicating the food laid out on the countertop. "As you can see, there's ham and cheese, lettuce and tomatoes, pickles and olives, chips and pretzels, mayo and mustard and bread and rolls." She moved her hand slightly to indicate the refrigerator. "I also bought small containers of potato and macaroni salad, as well."

"You *were* shopping," Royce said over a low, appreciative grumble from his empty stomach.

Evidently hearing the noise, Megan laughed and moved closer to the counter, and the cutting board she had placed there in readiness. "If you'll tell me what you want on your sandwich, I'll make it for you."

"Ham, cheese, lettuce, tomato and mayo on a roll," Royce recited. "Pickles, olives, chips and potato salad on the side." He raised one eyebrow. "What's to drink?"

"Decaffeinated coffee, tea, soda, beer, fruit juice, milk or water," Megan said, spreading butter on a kaiser roll. "The coffee's fresh, in the pot, and the other drinks are in the fridge. Help yourself."

"Are you going to join me in this repast?" he drawled, ambling to the refrigerator.

"Yes." Megan shot a quick grin at him. "I didn't eat much for dinner, either. I, er, wanted to get back to work."

"You have been busy," he murmured, returning her grin as he pulled the salad containers and the pickle and olive jars from the appliance. "Make any headway?"

"Yes." Megan's voice held a deep vein of satisfaction. "As a matter of fact, I finished the project, so this midnight snack is something of a celebration for me."

"Hey, that's great. Congratulations," Royce said, verbally applauding her. "So, what's on the agenda?" he asked, while continuing to gather together food, plates and glasses, then carry them to the table. "Another project?"

"Nope, nothing," Megan answered, turning away from the counter to frown at the table. "Do you want to bring those plates over here? The sandwiches are ready."

"Oh . . . sure," Royce said agreeably, ambling back to her side with the plates. "Looks good," he told her, his mouth watering at the sight of the food. "You build a mean-looking sandwich, lady."

"Thank you kindly, sir," Megan said solemnly. Then she went on, impishly. "So, let's not stand here admiring them, let's demolish them."

And that was exactly what they did. And while they did, the conversation was reduced to a minimum.

"Actually, I do have one thing on my agenda," Megan said casually as they worked together clearing away afterward.

Alerted by the almost too casual note in her tone, Royce slanted a probing look at her. "Yeah, what's that?"

"I stopped by the dealership on Commerce Avenue on my way home from the supermarket," she said, slowly.

"And?" He arched his brows.

Megan fidgeted with the dishcloth. "I, er, saw one model that I kinda liked."

"But?" he nudged.

Her fingers twisted the cloth. "But, um, I'd really appreciate another opinion. A man's opinion."

Royce grinned. "Mine?"

"If you wouldn't mind?" she asked, hopefully.

"Honey, I wouldn't mind at all," he assured her, feeling inordinately please by her request. "When would you like to go, tomorrow morning?"

"It already is tomorrow morning," she pointed out, appearing both relieved and as pleased as he felt.

"So it is," Royce conceded, glancing at the clock. "And time for me to get out of here and let you get to bed." Tamping down an impulse to take her into his arms and suggest they get to bed together, he moved to the kitchen doorway.

"I am sleepy," Megan admitted, trailing along the hallway behind him. "I didn't get much sleep last night."

Tell me about it, Royce thought, recalling his own discomfort the night before, both in the recliner and in his mind and body. Come to that, he reflected, turning to her when he reached the front door, the way she looked in that silky caftan was making him pretty damned uncomfortable right now.

"Ah, let's see," he said, shooting a look at his watch. "It's going on two. Suppose I pick you up around eleven-thirty? We can take a look at the car, then have lunch."

"Is your mind always on food?" she asked teasingly, her eyes bright with inner amusement.

Not hardly, Royce answered in silent longing, while aloud he replied, "No, not always." Unable to resist a sudden urge, he raised his hand to slowly brush his fingertips across her cheek to the corner of her mouth, his touch a light caress against the faint bruises marring the perfection of her creamy skin. Anger, hot and biting, for the man who had inflicted those bruises twisted inside Royce.

He kept the rage from coloring his voice by exerting all the control he possessed. "My mind is often on other things, Megan," he murmured.

"Wh-what kinds of things?"

The anger merged with desire. Royce felt a pang in his chest, a constriction in his throat. Megan's eyes were wide, luminous...vulnerable. He wanted, so very badly, to take her in his arms, cradle her, protect her, make love to her.

But he couldn't allow himself the pleasure that holding her, loving her, would give him. Because the pure light of trust also shone out of her eyes.

Megan trusted him; Royce would rather die than betray that trust.

"Maybe I'll tell you, someday," he replied, smothering a sigh as he drew his index finger over the sweet curve of her lower lip. "But not today."

"I... I don't understand," she said in a soft, plaintive little murmur.

"I know." Royce smiled, and let his hand fall away from her tempting mouth. "Hell, I'm not certain that I do." Shrugging, he turned to open the door. "I'll see you at eleven-thirty," he said, stepping into the cold night air. "Good night, Megan. Lock up tight. Sleep well."

Sleep well.

Fat chance.

Megan shifted position, again. Over an hour had passed since Royce had left her with those parting words, an hour in which she had continued to thrill to his tantalizing touch, while puzzling over his enigmatic remark.

My mind is often on other things...

What had he meant? What other things? Personal? Professional? Megan wondered. More important, did those unmentioned other things involve her in any way?

Excitement, uncertainty, confusion, were a mixed bag inside Megan's stomach.

She hoped, and feared to hope. She yearned, and was afraid of the yearning. She needed, and ...

And what?

Megan shifted position yet again, made uncomfortable and restless by her own thoughts.

But there were thoughts, emotions, desires and, yes, fears that had to be confronted and examined. Otherwise, Megan knew, there was a danger of closing herself off from any normal contact and association with members of the opposite sex.

Sex.

The word loomed in Megan's mind.

Intuition told her that the other things on Royce's mind were all directly related to that one word—intuition, and physical and emotional reactions.

Her lips burned with the imprint of Royce's caress.

Royce had touched her, in a sensuous, intimate manner, and she had not cringed, had not felt revulsion, had not been filled with stifling panic, as she had feared she would be upon ever again being touched by any man.

Quite the contrary. To Megan's utter surprise, she had responded to his caress, going all soft and quivery inside, breathless from the wonder of it all.

Physical attraction?

Sex?

In spades, she acknowledged. But it was more than mere sexual attraction—much, much more.

Megan wasn't as yet quite ready to delve into the depths of just what that much, much more entailed, but the shadow of it was there, hovering at the edges of her consciousness, haunting her as effectively as some persistent ghost.

The analogy brought a frown to Megan's brow. The day of reckoning would come, the day when she would have to face the truth of her feelings, emotions, fears and hopes.

But this wasn't that day. It was too soon, Megan told herself, absently raising her hand to smother a yawn. Maybe tomorrow, or the next day, she mused, curling onto her side as her eyelids drifted shut.

Maybe.

The ringing phone woke Royce at 8:14.

Groaning, he stretched out his arm, groping for the instrument set on the nightstand by the bed.

"'lo," he mumbled into the receiver around a wide, noisy yawn.

"Did I wake you?" The deep voice held a definite note of amusement.

"Naw," Royce replied, his lips twitching into a rueful smile. "I always sound like I have a mouth full of cotton in the morning." Blinking the sleep from his eyes, he shimmied up the bed to prop his shoulders against the headboard. "What's up, big bro?"

"Let's not go into that," Cameron drawled, eliciting a chuckle from his younger brother. "I was wondering if you had talked to Mother."

"Not in nearly a week," Royce said, a spark of alarm stealing the chuckle, and much of the moisture, from his throat. "Why? Is something wrong?"

"No, no. Don't go into a tailspin, Royce," Cameron hastened to assure him. "Mother's fine."

Royce let his breath out on a sigh of relief, before launching an attack. "Well, dammit, Cam, if everything's fine, why did you wake me up to ask me if I had talked to her? You had me close to a cold sweat."

"You always were the overconcerned one," Cameron said dryly. "Must get your mother-hen personality from the mother hen."

"You're a laugh a minute, you know that?" Royce retorted. "Now, if nothing's wrong at home, would you mind telling me the purpose for this inane call?"

"I am never inane, little brother." Cameron's voice contained both steel and utter conviction.

The damn thing was, his brother's statement was as solid as the Rock of Gibraltar, Royce silently conceded. The bottom line was that if Cameron said something was so, then it was so.

"I know, I know," Royce admitted. "But cut me a break, will ya? I'm not quite with it."

"Tell me about it," Cam taunted.

Royce sighed. "Look, Ca-me-ron," he said, in tones of rigidly imposed patience. "I worked the late shift. I didn't get to bed until 2:30. I want to get back to sleep. Did you call me for a real reason, or just to see if I was still here?"

Cameron laughed.

Royce decided it would be very easy to actively dislike his older brother...if he didn't practically worship the very ground Cam set his size twelves upon.

"Okay, here's the scoop." Cameron's voice was now brisk, if still overlaid with amusement. "Jake's in love."

"I'll alert the media," Royce retorted, yawning loudly into the mouthpiece. "But I already knew. For crying out loud, Cam, Mother told me about Jake way back last fall, and has been giving me periodic updates ever since."

"I'm talking *seriously* in love, Royce."

"Well, hell, I figured that," Royce said. "Didn't I just say Mom's been keeping me posted?"

"I mean, *marriage* serious," Cameron said. "Did you know that?"

"Marriage?" Royce sat bolt upright.

"Appears so."

"When?" Royce stared in bemusement at the opposite wall, seeing an image of his youngest brother with his inner eye. Jake, the baby, was getting married?

"Late spring." Cameron's soft laughter conveyed amusement and indulgence. "Seems we're going to have a June wedding."

"I'll be damned," Royce murmured.

"Likely, but that's beside the point," Cameron drawled. "Mother will probably be calling with the news any minute now. Act surprised, will you? She's waited a long time for a wedding in the family, and I don't want to ruin her fun. I do hate to steal her thunder."

"Yeah, sure," Royce agreed vaguely, distracted by the image of young Jake traipsing down the proverbial aisle. "I'll give her an award-winning performance."

"Thanks." Cameron was quiet a moment, and then he asked, "So, what do you think about it?"

Royce frowned. What did he think about it? "I don't know. I haven't decided yet." He shrugged, then laughed. "Do you think Jake gives a damn what I think...or what you and Eric think, come to that?"

"No, and rightly so," Cameron said, laughing with him.

"Right," Royce concurred. "I've been curious about Sarah ever since Mom told me about her. Now I can't wait to meet her."

"Well, you won't have to wait too long. You'll be meeting her at the gathering of the Wolfe pack in June." Cameron's voice turned brisk. "I've got to go, I've got another call. You can go back to sleep now, Royce. Talk to you later."

"Yeah, later, bro."

Marriage.

The word stood, bold as brass, in the forefront of Royce's mind, barring a return to slumber. There was a lot of tossing, a lot of heaving his long frame from one position to another position, but no escape into sleep.

"Damn."

Cursing beneath his breath, Royce finally gave up the battle and crawled out from under the tangled covers on his king-size bed.

Marriage. And Jake. The youngest of the four Wolfe progeny; the first to take the plunge into matrimony.

Who would have thunk it?

Shaking his head in bemusement, Royce left the bedroom, heading for what he hoped would be a reviving shower.

Marriage.

The word seemed to get stuck in a mental groove, revolving and repeating inside Royce's head while he wallowed in a long, leisurely, stinging-hot shower.

The one-word refrain persisted as he made faces at himself in the bathroom mirror, contorting to find and scythe every tiny trace of morning stubble.

He was picking up Megan for car-looking and lunch.

After selecting, then discarding, several combinations of pants, shirt and sport jacket, and eventually settling on the fifth ensemble he put together, Royce wandered into the minuscule kitchen in his apartment to make a pot of coffee.

But would lunchtime ever come?

The clock on the stove read 10:17.

Royce exhaled a deep sigh; almost an hour to kill before he could leave to pick up Megan.

In the interim, Royce polished off two pots of coffee and a hearty number of slightly stale English muffins. Toasting eliminated the staleness. After eating, he filled in the remaining minutes cleaning up the kitchen, making his bed and rehanging his clothes in the bedroom, and tidying up the living room—which didn't take long, since it was only marginally larger than the minuscule kitchen, and a great deal smaller than the spacious bedroom.

Which just went to prove that, in the case of space allocation, Royce had his priorities straight.

When, at last, Royce strode from his apartment, he felt he now knew precisely the feelings of a felon being sprung from the slammer.

Marriage.

Though less bold, thus less demanding of his immediate attention, the word was there, comfortably ensconced at the back of his mind.

All in relation to Jake...of course.

The day was fine, the breeze cool but scented with the promise of spring, hovering just around the corner.

Megan was waiting for Royce on the front stoop, her face raised to the strengthening warmth of the sunlight. Smiling, she drew in a deep breath, trying to capture the elusive scent teasing her senses. Her smile curved into a frown at the discordant sound of a bad car muffler disturbing the late morning peace and tranquillity.

The crunching noise had a familiar ring.

Now, where . . .

Megan's emerging thoughts took flight as a dark green car made a smooth, purring turn into her driveway.

Royce.

Thinking his name brought a flutter to her pulse, a soaring sense of joy skittering throughout her being. Her lips curved into a bright smile of pleasure at the sight of him.

The effect on Royce was gratifying, to say the least.

He looked stunned, bemused, bewitched. He also appeared incapable of movement. Bringing the car to a stop alongside her, he simply sat, staring into her smiling face.

Laughter bubbled up Megan's throat and over her lips. The sound of her amusement dancing on the mild spring air, she opened the passenger-side door and slid onto the seat next to him, her laughter taking on a teasing note.

"Cat got your tongue?" Megan asked when he just sat there, staring at her.

"No," Royce said in somber seriousness. "Your smile stole my breath."

His bold admission rendered Megan as speechless as he had been. For an eternity of seconds, they merely sat there, staring into each other's eyes.

The flutter in Megan's pulses accelerated into a thundering gallop that thrummed in every nerve ending. Her breath was shallow, her heartbeat deep.

She suddenly ached... everywhere.

The exquisite pain shattered her trancelike state.

"Ah..." Megan paused, swallowed, cleared her throat. "I guess we'd better get going."

Royce released his visual lock on her with flattering reluctance. "Yeah." His voice was strained, ragged; his fingers betrayed a fine tremor when he reached for the key in the ignition.

The engine fired, and he slanted a glance at her. Then, drawing a deep breath, he set the car into motion.

Megan sat, still and contemplative, throughout the drive to the car dealership. Not knowing quite what to think of the strange interlude they had shared, she tried not to think about it at all.

But that didn't work, because she could still see his eyes, the bright blue darkened by emotion.

It was all very thrilling... and rather scary. Scary enough to keep her quiet, thinking, while trying not to think.

Apparently Royce was experiencing similar difficulties, for he remained as quiet as Megan.

Shopping for a new car was decidedly anticlimactic. Royce approved the silver-gray sports car, and Megan made arrangements to buy it. It was all cut-and-dried.

After becoming lost inside blue eyes intent on peering into her soul, Megan could hardly feel thrilled by the prospect of becoming the owner of what, in fact, was nothing more than a piece of metal with wheels.

The sports car was beautiful, but inanimate.

Royce Wolfe was real.

Now *that* was something to think about.

And Megan did think about it, long after Royce had driven her back to the house after lunch, through the even longer afternoon, and into the silence of the night.

She thought about nothing else except Royce until the silence of the night was broken by the innocent-sounding ring of the telephone.

Certain it was Royce, Megan snatched up the receiver and blurted out a breathless "Hello?"

"I'm coming for you, bitch."

Megan's breath ceased at the familiar sound of the harsh voice—the haunting sound of her attacker. Panic clutched at her throat; fear froze her in place.

"And when I get there, I'm going to..."

Megan's stomach roiled, threatening to reject her light supper, at the obscene description the man spewed out of what he was planning to do to her.

The sour taste of bile filled her mouth, and with a whimpered protest Megan slammed down the receiver. Terrified, sobbing, she grabbed it up again and punched in the number Royce had given to her so that she could reach him at work.

"Sergeant Wolfe," he answered on the second ring.

"Royce!" Megan cried, her voice high with rising hysteria. "He's coming for me. That man, that hulking man, he's coming for me. He said... he said..."

"I'm on my way."

The line went dead.

Caught in the gripping claws of fear, Megan stood, the telephone receiver pressed to her breast, afraid to move, her body shaking, waiting for deliverance.

Royce.

Nine

"Megan!"

The razor-edged sound of Royce's voice, overlapping a sharply delivered rapping against the front door, pierced the fear-induced trance holding Megan's mind captive.

A shudder of awareness quaked through her. The phone falling away from her nerveless fingers, she whirled and ran from the bedroom to the foyer. His call rang out again as she dashed across the chill flagstone inlay to the door.

"*Me-gan.*"

There was now a new note in his voice, a note she had not previously heard before, a note rife with abject, unadulterated fright.

"I'm here," she called in immediate response. "I'm all right," she hastened to assure him.

Fumbling with the lock, Megan shoved to the back of her mind the intriguing speculation on the possible meaning for the sound of sheer panic coloring his tone.

"Open the damn door," he ordered.

"I'm ... I'm trying!" Megan heaved a sigh of relief as the lock gave way. Cranking the knob, she stepped back and pulled the door open.

This time, she did not fling herself against him. She could not, for with the first opening crack in the doorway Royce strode inside and swept her into his arms, crushing her to his tension-taut body.

Safe. Safe.

The words repeated inside Megan's mind as she clung to the solid strength of the man she now trusted without question or doubt.

But even Royce's solid strength revealed the ravages of emotional fear. Locked within that uncompromising embrace, Megan could not help but notice the fine tremor shivering through his long frame. In truth, she could barely tell which of them was trembling more, she herself or Royce.

"I want you to tell me exactly what happened." Even his voice betrayed his inner unsteadiness.

"At first ... when I answered the phone, there was nothing, just silence," Megan said shakily, tilting her head back to look up, into his sternly set face. "But then ... then," she went on, her voice gathering speed and panic as she continued, "he called me 'bitch' and said he was going to..." She broke off, eyes widening, then cried, "Royce, he knows who I am! He knows where I am! He's coming here to... to... He intends to finish what he started last Friday night!"

"Like hell he will." Royce released her with confusing abruptness. "You're getting out of here."

"But...oh!" Megan exclaimed, starting when he grasped her hand and literally yanked her along with him as he strode into her bedroom.

"Where's your bag?"

"Bag?" Megan blinked. "Wha—"

"Suitcase, carryon, garment bag." Keeping a tight hold on her hand, he moved to the double closet set into the bathroom wall. "Anything to throw a few things into."

"But...but..."

"Dammit, Megan," Royce exploded, whipping around to pin her with blue eyes blazing with impatience and flat-out fury. "Don't stand there sputtering at me like a motorboat running out of fuel. I'm getting you out of here. Now. You can think of it as protective custody. Where do you keep your bags?"

"On the shelf in that closet," she said, flicking her free hand at the double doors. "But where are you taking me?" she demanded. "To the lockup?"

"The lockup?" Royce gave her a sour look, then turned toward the closet doors. "Get real, Megan," he said, releasing her hand to pull the doors open. "Get some things together and get dressed." He pulled her nylon carryon from the shelf and thrust it into her hands. "I'm taking you to my place."

His place.

Megan stood in the center of the small living room, feeling nervous, uncertain, and rather ridiculous.

She wasn't even properly dressed, for pity's sake, she thought, clutching her full-length wool coat to her shivering body as she glanced around her.

Beneath the coat, all Megan had on was the night-shirt she'd been wearing when that terrible person called, a pair of sweatpants she had pulled on under the shirt, and low-heeled, soft leather slip-ons she had barely had time to slip on before Royce hustled her out of the house and into his car.

Megan was cold, a condition attributable more to her emotional state than to the outside air temperature of forty degrees or so. This chill was inside, not outside.

Still, she huddled beneath the coat, seeking comfort from the warming wool.

"You can relax now," Royce murmured, shucking out of his jacket. "You're safe." Tossing the jacket aside, he slowly walked to her, coming to a stop mere inches from her.

"Yes." Megan managed a smile, faint but real, for him. "Thank you, Royce."

"You're welcome." His answering smile was tender, compassionate, understanding. "You can take your coat off now."

"I…" Megan shivered and wet her lips. "I'm cold."

"I know, but the coat won't contain the chill." He held out his hand. "And you know it."

Megan drew a quick breath, hesitated, then raised her trembling fingers to the coat buttons. It seemed to take forever to unfasten the four plain black buttons. Royce didn't try to help her or hurry her. He stood there, quiet and patient, until the coat's panels gaped apart. After she removed the garment and handed it to him, he turned away to carefully drape it over the back of an oversize—Royce-size—club chair.

The minute the coat was off, Megan wished she had it back. Her shiver intensified into a teeth-rattling tremble.

"R-R-Royce," she began, her muscles clenching against the reactionary shakes. "I—need…"

Suddenly Royce was there, drawing her into his arms, taking the place of the coat, enfolding her within the warmer cocoon of his presence.

"I know, I know," he whispered, his breath ruffling wisps of hair at her temple. "But it's all right now." He stroked one hand down the length of her spine. "You're all right now." His lips brushed from the corner of her eyebrow to her quivering cheek. "I won't let him, or anyone else, hurt you, Megan. Depend on it."

Clutching him every bit as tightly as she had clutched her coat, Megan burrowed against him, into him, seeking the strength of his body, as well as his conviction.

The chill permeating her body slowly lessened. And still she trembled, but now the tremors were activated by a shiver of unvarnished sensual awareness of him.

His soft voice dissolved her fears; his stroking hands unlocked her clenched muscles; his caressing lips ignited a fire that consumed her.

Slowly, but inevitably, like a tightly closed early-spring bud, Megan responded to Royce's caring ministrations, unfolding like the flower in the warmth of the sun.

"You will stay here, with me, safe from harm, for as long as it takes," he murmured, the light movement of his mouth on her cheek causing ripples of sensation from her face to the outer edges of her tingling toes.

Megan didn't need to ask what he meant; though he hadn't said so, she knew he meant she was to stay with him until her attacker was apprehended and confined.

"I...I can't. I don't expect you to..." She broke off on a softly gasped "Oh!"

His lips had drifted to the corner of her mouth. "I know," he said, tantalizing her lips with the feather-light touch of his mouth. "I want to do this, keep you safe, protected, for myself, my sanity, as well as for your peace of mind."

Peace of mind! Megan quivered. At that moment, her mind was anything but at peace—not to mention her senses! Her mind was a chaotic whirl, her senses running riot.

His nearness, his unmistakable arousal, the allure of his mouth, were playing havoc with every feminine impulse Megan possessed.

Royce continued to murmur words of comfort and reassurance that she no longer heard. All her powers of concentration were centered on his lips, teasing the edges of her own.

Suddenly, the world of harsh reality retreated, banished by the forward charge of the realm of sensuality. Her overriding priority was the compulsion to taste his mouth.

A whimper shuddering from the depths of her throat, Megan turned her head, bringing her lips into contact with the mouth she craved.

"Megan?" Royce's voice could only have been described as raw. "You're understandably upset." He drew another soft whimper from her as he raised his head to stare into her eyes. "Are you certain this is what you want?"

A firm affirmation sprang to her lips, just as a startling thought sprang into her mind. The thought spilled from her mind to her tongue.

"Are you afraid I just want to use you to forget?" she asked, biting her lower lip in consternation.

The glow that deepened the blue of his eyes, and the smile that drifted across his lips presaged his answer.

"Honey, feel free to use me for anything. A hand to hang on to, a buffer against fear, an opinion on the choice of a car—" his voice went low, intimate, sexy "—a body to warm you, soothe you, fulfill you."

"Royce." Megan's voice was barely there, so she let her eyes speak of her needs.

"Use me, honey," he murmured, slowly lowering his head, his mouth, to hers. "Please, please, use me."

His lips touched hers, tentatively, testingly, sweetly. Megan shuddered from the thistledown impact.

Gentle. His kiss was the most gentle blending of two mouths imaginable. And seductive. Royce's very gentleness seduced not Megan's body, but her mind.

Feeling utterly safe, secure within the warm haven of his embrace, she divorced herself from concern, and surrendered her being into his care.

Royce moved; Megan moved with him.

Lost inside the blue heaven of his eyes, she didn't notice the details of his bedroom, or even the kingly size of his bed. She didn't notice the coolness of the air against her bare skin when he carefully removed her nightshirt, her sweatpants and her panties.

The mattress was firm, a solid support for a big man. Megan didn't notice that, either. She was too fascinated with watching Royce undress to take note.

He was a beautiful sight in the natural state. She could not discern an ounce of excess weight on his long, muscular body. His shoulders and lightly haired chest were broad, his waist and hips were narrow, his belly was flat, and his long legs were straight and well shaped.

His fully aroused manhood was of a size scaled to the rest of his body.

The overall effect of him was formidable.

Megan suffered a twinge of disquiet.

"Easy, Megan, easy," he murmured, stretching his length out next to her on the bed. "I'm not a boy, or an animal. I will not clutch, or grab." Shifting to his side facing her, he stroked her shoulder, her arm, the back of her hand, her fingers.

Megan felt his feather-light touch in the depths of her being—felt it and responded to it.

"I'm...I'm not afraid," she said, secretly willing away the tiny flare of trepidation.

"Of course you are, and understandably so." His eyes and smile were soft with compassion, and a hint of sadness. "I want to make love with you, Megan, probably more than I have ever wanted anything else before in my entire adult life." He drew a deep, shuddering breath. "But I have nothing to prove here, no issues to resolve." Acceptance now tinged his tone. "Say the word, anytime, and I'll back off. I can live with frustration. I could not bear living with the thought of having frightened or hurt you in any way."

"Oh, Royce." Thoroughly reassured, and disarmed, Megan blinked away the sting of tears in her eyes, and raised her hands to cup his face to draw his mouth to hers. "Come to me," she whispered against his lips. "Make love with me."

Royce was incredibly gentle. Even so, memory sparked and Megan tensed when he eased into position between her thighs.

He went still. His hands braced at either side of her head, he stared into her eyes a moment, then began slowly to withdraw from her.

"No." Megan shook her head, and clasped his hips, holding him in place. "I'm all right. It's all right."

He frowned. "Are you sure?"

"Yes. I trust you, Royce. I'd trust you with my life." She managed a smile. "I know I can trust you with my body."

"Yes. You can," he said. "I swear it."

And he proceeded to prove his assertion.

Slowly, and with infinite care, Royce brought himself to her, joining his body with hers in gentle possession. His mouth claimed hers, and then, in unison, his body and tongue stroked in ever-increasing thrusts, fanning the flames of desire into a blaze raging out of control.

Megan experienced a different form of tension, a spiraling, crackling tension born of sensual excitement. Suddenly, she felt as though she *were* the flame, burning brightly for him, only for Royce.

There was no past. There was no future. There was only the here, and the now, the instant, striving for the next instant, and then the next, toward the ultimate goal of perfect harmony, complete freedom. Oneness.

The ultimate attained, Megan cried out in sheer wonder at the beauty of the moment. Royce's hoarse-voiced exclamation echoed her own.

* * *

He might have made a very costly mistake.

Royce stood in the bedroom doorway, his expression pensive, his feelings in conflict, as he stared at the woman asleep in his bed.

In the cold, clear light of midmorning, the smoky haze of last night's passion took on a different and unsettling hue. He had slept better, deeper, than he had in nearly a year. But what, he mused, was that sleep going to cost him?

A sigh expanded his chest as he stared bleakly into the sleeping woman's face.

Megan looked so vulnerable, so defenseless, so gut-wrenchingly appealing, in slumber. It took all his considerable control to keep from going to her, joining her on the bed, losing himself in the joy of loving her.

Loving Megan.

There it was, the root cause for the messed-up condition of his thought processes.

When had the wanting turned into love?

Royce released the pent-up sigh.

What did when, or even why matter?

He was in love with her.

The acknowledgment scared the hell out of him.

Megan sighed in her sleep. A soft smile curved her lips. Then a whisper hit him with the force of a scream.

"Royce."

He winced at the beguiling sound of his name on her lips. He knew he had satisfied her, in a physical sense. But had he touched her emotionally, engaged her affections?

Did Megan care for him in any meaningful way?

The question kept him standing in the doorway, wanting to go to her, yet hesitant, afraid the answer might turn out to be the one he didn't want to hear.

Big tough cop. Royce derided himself. If your brothers could see you now, he mused, they'd laugh themselves sick.

That didn't matter, either. Hell, it was easy to be tough professionally. On the job, his emotions weren't involved. Well, as a rule his emotions weren't involved.

Megan just happened to be a special case, with the potential to turn *him* into a basket case.

Royce had been close to being in love before, and had been rejected. It had hurt like hell. Now, after nearly a year, he knew the blow had been mainly to his pride, his ego. He also knew that his feelings for Megan were different, deeper, permanent.

If he declared himself to Megan, and she rejected him, he would be devastated. Royce knew that, as well.

She murmured his name again in her sleep.

Royce backed away from the doorway, calling himself a coward with each retreating step.

Later, he justified his action—or lack of same. Megan had endured a traumatizing ordeal. She needed time to heal, not more emotional baggage to weigh her down—and most especially not *his* emotional baggage.

But, damn, not knowing how she felt, whether or not she cared, was tearing him apart.

Megan woke feeling vaguely disoriented, dissatisfied and definitely disgruntled.

A quick glance around her clarified her disorientation. She was ensconced in Royce's bed. Determining her sense of place clarified her dissatisfaction. What she and Royce had shared had been wonderful—and she wanted more of it. The acknowledgment of need clarified the disgruntlement. She was building up a head of angry steam.

Damn that hulking man, Megan fumed, tossing back the rumpled covers. Damn that attacker of women, for casting her in the role of victim, a supplicant for protection from the one man she could give herself to completely and unconditionally.

Railing against the unfairness of it all, she scooped her nightshirt from the floor and stormed into the bathroom.

Megan's mind spun its wheels the entire time required to shower and shampoo.

Making love with Royce had been more than wonderful; it had been everything she had ever dared fantasize being intimate with a man could be. In point of fact, it had been even more than that, for, with absolute honesty, Megan knew that she had been more than making love with Royce; she was deeply in love with him. And the more she thought about it, the angrier she became.

Her ire at full arousal, Megan stormed back into the bedroom, collecting her carry-on bag from the living room as she whirled through.

Her blood heating to a roiling boil as she hastily dressed in slacks and a loose-knit midthigh-length sweater, Megan continued to mentally lash out at the fate that had placed her in her present predicament.

After years—and men—that had been totally discouraging, she had finally found the man who embodied every one of her secret dreams of the ideal partner—kind, caring, compassionate, intelligent, humorous, and sexy as the very devil.

And Megan loved Royce. Of course she loved him. She was destined to love him.

Dammit, she protested, against her situation and against the tug of the brush she yanked through her tangled hair.

She loved, but... Megan gritted her teeth. But because of that... that thing who dared to impersonate a man, she was very much afraid that the driving force behind Royce's response to her owed more to the kind of man he was, the embodiment of all his fine qualities, than to his loving her in return.

But Megan couldn't know Royce's thoughts or feelings. She did know that he had not once so much as hinted at, never mind mentioned, love.

And therein lay the cause of the anger eating away at her, anger directed not at Royce, but at that despicable hulking man whose presence overshadowed every facet of her life.

Well, enough was enough, Megan decided, stamping into ankle boots. She was done with cowering and hiding.

She wanted her life back.

She wanted Royce.

First things first.

Where was Royce, anyway?

The phone rang as Megan left the bedroom.

Following the muted sound of his voice, Megan crossed through the living room and came to a halt in the kitchen doorway. Royce stood with his back to her, his shoulder resting against the wall, talking on the phone.

Lord, he looked gorgeous.

"You're kidding."

Megan noted the surprise in his voice, but really didn't pay too much attention to what he was saying. She was too distracted by the effect of the sight of him, his powerful effect on her senses.

Merely looking at him made her feel all hot and melty inside, and all shivery outside.

Love? Megan was hard-pressed to keep from laughing out loud, and not in genuine amusement. She was suffering every one of the classic symptoms.

Love?

In spades.

"A June wedding, huh?"

That snagged her attention. Megan's ears perked up. A June wedding sounded perfect.

"Are you serious? Of course I'll be able to make it. I'll put in a request for vacation for the first week in June, when I go back to work tomorrow."

Tomorrow? Megan frowned.

"Yeah, Mom, I'll take care." Royce shifted away from the wall. "You too. And pass along my congratulations to Jake. Tell him I can't wait to meet Sarah." He chuckled. "She's got to be some kind of woman, if she's willing to take on the job of housebreaking that maverick."

Megan's frown melted into a smile at the underlying note of true affection in Royce's tone. The evidence of his love for his family was unvarnished, and unashamedly voiced.

She liked that in a man.

Royce turned as he hung up the receiver, and caught sight of Megan's misty smile.

"Hi." His voice was now low, intimate.

Megan felt a responsive thrill; it affected her own voice, making it throaty. "Hi."

"Sleep well?" While his voice remained low and even, his eyes bored into hers with intent.

"Yes." Megan's frown crept back to steal her smile. "Did you?"

"Oh, yeah, terrific." His reply came too quickly, and was much too glib. But he turned away before she could question him on it. "There's fresh coffee," he said, going to the tiny counter next to the sink. "Are you hungry?"

"No." Megan shook her head, even though he couldn't see her. "I'll just have coffee, thank you." She hesitated, bit down on her lip, then blurted out, "Royce, what's wrong? Are you sorry about last night?"

Ten

"Sorry?" Royce whipped around to stare at her. "No, I'm not sorry, but..." He shrugged.

But. Megan felt a sick sensation in her stomach. It was the *buts* in life that did you in.

"I see." Somehow, she managed to keep the pain from spilling over into her voice.

"No, I don't think you do." Royce gave a sharp shake of his head. "Megan, honey, it's this damnable situation. You're so fragile right now, so vulnerable, and..." He paused, as if groping for just the right words.

She didn't give him time to find them. Mentally backing away from the abyss of unthinkable pain, she put on her brightest morning face.

"I know, I know." She flicked her hand, dismissing the subject. "I couldn't help overhearing part of your telephone conversation," she went on, rapid-fire. "Your brother is getting married?"

"Huh?" He frowned, then, shifting mental gears, caught up with her. "Oh. Yes. That was my mother on the phone. Jake and his lady have set the date to take the fatal step on the first Saturday in June."

The fatal step. Megan's spirits took a nosedive. His phrasing said just about all there was to say concerning his opinion of the marital state. Or was he simply trying to tell her something, something direct and personal? Well, so much for hopes and dreams and fantasies.

Keeping her bright morning face in place was growing more difficult by the second. "That's nice. I, er, hope they'll be very happy." She smothered a sigh and worked up a faint smile of thanks for the cup of steaming coffee he poured for her. "Did I also hear you say something about not having to work today?" She raised the cup to her lips, and her eyebrows in what she hoped was an expression of casual interest.

Royce nodded. "Today and tomorrow are my scheduled days off." He paused an instant, then went on. "But I have to go out for a while. I have some things to do."

Recognizing opportunity when it stared her in the face, Megan grabbed for it.

"Do you? Well, I'm going to call the car dealer to ask if my car's ready for me," she said offhandedly.

"If it is, would you please drop me off there, so I can pick it up? And if it isn't," she rushed on, "would you drop me at home?"

"No." Flat. Unequivocal. Final.

"No?" Megan had never taken well to flat, unequivocal and final. "I beg your pardon?"

"I don't want you going back to the house." Royce's features were locked into an expression of stern determination.

"But I must go home," she argued. "I brought only one change of clothes with me. Besides, I have to package my illustrations for mailing and get them to the post office."

"No, Megan." He slowly shook his head. "It's not safe for you to go back there. If you'll tell me what clothing you'll need, and how you want the illustrations packaged, I'll take care of everything for you."

Indeed? Though Megan kept the biting response inside her head, it burned like fiery anger on her tongue. But the bitter anger was directed more at herself than at him—even if he was getting a tad too heavy-handed.

Royce had been wonderful from the beginning—taking care of everything since that dreadful night. From standing by in the hospital to driving her home, then stopping by every night to check up on her, he had been there for her. He had gone way beyond the call of duty.

And Megan had greedily availed herself of his offer to use his body to lose herself. She had used him shamelessly, she admitted to herself in all honesty. She had used him eagerly, joyously, wantonly. She had used him for all he was worth—and in the process, she had returned his generous offer by giving freely of herself, for all she was worth, body, mind and soul.

Megan loved Royce, was now deeply in love with him, but acknowledged that Royce could in no way be faulted if he did not love her in return.

If.

Megan clung to the word. To her way of thinking, so long as there was an if, there was a hope, a hope to build a friendship, a relationship, and possibly even a mutual and deeply committed love, upon.

But—the dreaded but—first she had to reclaim her independence, her life, the way it had been before that beast posing as a man robbed her of it.

And to begin with, Megan was done with running—literally, as well as figuratively. Lifting her chin to a defiant angle, she stared Royce directly in the eyes.

"I *am* going," she said distinctly.

Royce was noticeably unimpressed by her show of bravado. His blue eyes placid, he stared right back at her.

"For*get* it," he told her, mimicking her tone. "I will not allow you to place yourself in harm's way."

"Really?" Megan arched one auburn eyebrow. "How are you planning to stop me?"

That gave him pause, but only for a few moments of visible frustration. Then he smiled. It sent an apprehensive shiver up her spine.

"I could take you into protective custody, citing fear for your life. Or I could take a different but equally effective route, and simply handcuff you to something solid, out of reach of a phone." His smile tilted, much too engagingly. "But I'd much prefer to have your word to me that you won't leave the apartment."

Mulling over whether or not he actually could legally confine her, Megan made a performance of considering the options he'd presented to her. Then she heaved a loud, defeated-sounding sigh of surrender.

"Okay, Wolfe, you win."

"You'll stay put?"

Loath to commit herself verbally with an outright lie, she nodded her head once in agreement.

"Say it, Megan." His voice was pure steel.

She glared at him in sheer disgruntlement at his persistence. He stared back. Seconds ticked by, and then she again gave way, while crossing the first two fingers of her free hand in childish self-exoneration.

"Okay, okay, I'll stay put."

Royce maintained his steely regard for a few seconds longer. Then he smiled, stirring a sickening sensation of guilt inside Megan. "Okay," he said, extending his hand, palm up. "If you'll give me your door key, I'll get to it."

Chagrin washed over her; she hadn't thought about the necessity of relinquishing her key. Fortunately, she then recollected the spare key her father kept hidden in the garage for just such contingencies. Her sense of chagrin evaporated in the warmth of her smile.

"I'll get it," she said, placing her cup on the table before turning to the doorway. "It's in my handbag."

"Can I get you something to eat before I leave?" Royce called after her.

"No, thank you," she called back. "I'm still not hungry. I'll have something later."

"Okay. Feel free to rummage through the fridge and cabinets." There was a pause, and then he called out again. "Megan, make a list of the clothes you want me to gather for you."

Even though she felt certain she wouldn't need them, at least not here, Megan dutifully pulled a notebook from her purse and jotted down an assortment of casual garments. Then, after unfastening the door key from the case, which also held the garage key, she left the bedroom.

Royce was waiting for her at the front door. "The sooner I get moving, the sooner I'll get back," he said, once again extending his hand, palm up.

Crossing to him, Megan placed the key and the scrap of paper in his palm, then launched into instructions on exactly how she wanted her illustrations packaged.

"Will do." He hesitated, as if unsure. Then, bending quickly to her, he brushed his lips over hers, murmuring, "Be good."

Megan felt bereft when he raised his head, and lonely the second the door closed behind him. Her lips tingling, hungry for more of his kisses, she stood staring bleakly at the solid panel, agonizing over the possibility that what she was about to do could cause an irreparable rift between them.

But she had to do it, Megan assured herself, bolstering her courage. She had to assert herself, make her own decisions, take back control of her existence.

Swinging away from the door, she went directly to the phone and punched in the number of the car dealership. If her car was ready, she would have to walk there to take possession, but needs must be met. Besides, it was a small town, after all, and the dealership was located only a little more than a mile from Royce's apartment.

The car was ready. Megan hung up the receiver. A satisfied smile curving her lips, she headed for the bathroom to apply some color to her face. It was to be the old shoe-leather express, but that was okay, she told herself. She could do with the exercise.

The day was mild, the air faintly scented with the elusive fragrance of early spring. Megan strode forward, looking for all the world as if she didn't have a care. In reality, she raked her eyes over each and every male she passed on the street, searching for, and yet fearful of spotting a large, hulking form looming up before her.

There were no hulking forms... or dark-browed males.

Megan's step faltered as she strode onto the car lot. Dark-browed males? Now why had she thought...?

A vision flashed into her mind, and she could see her attacker, clearly defined as he arced over her in the car, his lips curled into a snarl, his eyes narrowed and mean beneath lowered dark brows.

And she felt positive she would recognize him if she saw him again!

Megan shivered, and felt grateful for the sight of the salesman, a broad smile creasing his rather homely face, raising his arm in greeting as he hurried to meet her.

Mere minutes were required to dispense with the paperwork, during which Megan's attention was diverted from thoughts of mean eyes and dark brows to the more pleasurable and exciting prospects of a sparkling new sports car.

The formalities over with, Megan slipped into the contoured seat behind the steering wheel, gave a final wave to the grinning salesman and fired the engine.

It purred like a well-fed tiger.

Megan's spirits purred along with it. Taking it slow and cautious, she eased the silver beauty to the lot's driveway, inching forward as she checked the roadway for oncoming traffic. There was a string of vehicles coming toward her.

Waiting patiently, she began to hum, but the sound dried on her lips as a niggling memory sprang to life at another, discordant sound—a rattling muffler on a car midway in the line of oncoming cars.

Frowning in concentration, Megan peered through the windshield at the badly dented car. The sight of the driver of the car, viewed in profile, caused a burst of memory that sent fingers of panic curling around her throat.

It was him! Megan knew it as surely as she knew her own name. Suddenly she recalled taking note of the noisy car the first time she had visited the dealer, feeling a vague uneasiness about the look of the driver.

Without thought or hesitation, Megan pulled the sports car into the end of the line, determined to follow the rattling junker to its destination.

One by one, the other cars in the string turned off, until only one car remained between Megan and her target, which was headed on a direct course for her parents' home.

Her nerves feeling as if they were literally jumping wildly beneath her skin, Megan clutched the steering wheel with sweaty hands and maintained a discreet distance from the battered and noisy vehicle.

She felt sick to her stomach, and wanted nothing so much as to whip the sports car into a U-turn and beat a hasty retreat to the safety of Royce's apartment.

Royce. Thinking of him brought his mission to mind. He had said he had some things to do, but he had also promised to stop by the house to pack her illustrations and collect clothing for her. Maybe Royce was at the house now.

Distracted by her thoughts, Megan wasn't aware of the truck cutting her off at an intersection until it was almost on top of her. Reacting automatically, she sheered away from the large vehicle, avoiding a collision by a hairbreadth.

Shaken and trembling, she pulled to the side of the road and sat, still gripping the wheel, gulping in deep, composure-restoring breaths, while the driver of the truck went merrily on his way, unaware that he had come within mere seconds of wiping her off the face of the earth.

It wasn't until a measure of her calm was restored that Megan was struck by the realization that she had lost sight of the rattling car she had been tailing.

How long, she wondered, had she been sitting there, collecting her composure? Five minutes? Ten? Longer? As long as twenty minutes? She had to get moving. If Royce was at the house, and that man was headed there...

"Damn." Muttering the curse aloud, she set the car in motion again, and drove at a careful yet steady pace the rest of the distance to her parents' home.

Megan spotted the battered car again when she was less than a city block's distance from her destination. She couldn't miss it, for it was moving at speed, along the driveway, heading away from the house.

She took in the scene and comprehended its portent at once. The driver, the man she was now certain was her attacker, was on the run, fleeing from another man, who was at that moment diving into a distinctive dark green car parked to one side of the double garage.

"Royce!" Megan cried, knowing he couldn't hear her, knowing, as well, that, though officially off duty, he was in pursuit of a suspect—and the suspect had a head start.

The battered car was nearing the end of the driveway that Megan was approaching. And so she did the only thing she could think of to do. Without a qualm, she stamped down on the gas pedal. The silver sports car responded like an Indy race car. The purr accelerating into a growl, it shot forward, a silver streak aimed at intersecting the rattling junker.

With a cool she hadn't previously realized she possessed, Megan deliberately drove her brand-new car directly into the junker, crumpling the already battered front end.

The air bag deployed.

Though once again shaken, and slightly stunned, Megan was miraculously uninjured. She was performing the deep, composure-restoring routine when the door beside her was yanked open with a force nearly strong enough to tear it from its hinges and Royce thrust his head into the car.

"Dammit to hell, Megan, are you trying to kill yourself?" he shouted, directly into her face.

Recoiling from the assault on her ear drums, she tilted her body to the side, away from him. Then, realizing what she was doing, she shifted the other way, bringing her face so close to his that she could see the fine pores in his skin.

"No, I'm not trying to kill myself!" she shouted back at him. "I was trying to help you!"

There came the loud wail of a police car siren. Royce yelled above it.

"Help me? How? By hurting yourself?"

"I'm not hurt!" she yelled back.

"You gave me your word, Megan." Harsh accusation accented his raised voice.

"I crossed my fingers." The excuse sounded lame even to her own ears.

Royce made a disgusted face; it was not pretty. "You crossed your fingers," he repeated in a mutter. "Lord, I don't believe you." Shaking his head in despair, he straightened away from the car. "Are you sure you're all right?"

It was only then, as he stood back, that Megan noticed the reactive tremors cascading the length of his body. Feeling small, and not particularly bright, Megan nodded in answer. "What about him?" She turned to look at the man slumped over the wheel of the other car. "Maybe you'd better check on him."

Royce gave a sharp, backward jerk of his head as the patrolman came to a tire-screeching stop behind him. "Let the local law handle it. I'm off duty."

The local law officer did handle it, and very well at that. After assuring himself that Megan had not suffered any visible injuries, he proceeded to take charge of the situation.

Approaching the other vehicle apprehensively, Megan made a positive identification of the driver as the same man who had attacked her the previous Friday night.

Through it all, Royce stood by her side, close but withdrawn, asking no questions, offering no comments, making her nervous and fearful with his stoic silence.

The only time he spoke was when the patrolman told Megan she would have to go to the police station to file a criminal-assault complaint against the man.

"I'll drive her in," he said, immediately turning to walk to his car. "Let's get it over with, Megan."

There was something ominous, final-sounding, about his voice, his manner, that caused a queasy feeling in Megan's stomach, and a certainty in her mind that what he wanted to get over with involved more than the filing of a complaint.

Thanking the patrolman, Megan trailed after Royce, scared witless that with her rash action she had ruined the tenuous relationship they had begun.

"What about my car?" she asked, settling into the passenger seat beside him.

"The patrolman will have it towed."

His indifferent tone was less than encouraging. Nevertheless, Megan persevered. "You're really mad at me, aren't you?"

He shot a weary-looking glance at her. "Later, Megan." His voice was dull, flat with finality. "I don't want to talk about it here, en route to the police station."

"But... but I did help you catch that man!" Megan cried in her own defense.

"Yeah."

The disillusionment contained in that one small word effectively silenced her.

The formalities at the police station seemed endless, but finally Megan was told she could leave. Feeling wrung out, listless, and fighting a need to simply sit down and cry, she followed her still-silent escort to his car.

"I'll take you home now." Cynicism laced his tone. "Then we can talk about it."

Megan felt the bottom fall out of her tenuous hold on hope; his attitude did not bode well for the hours ahead, or the future, come to think of it.

The sports car was gone by the time they returned to the house, as was the rattler and its driver. Megan sighed as they made the swing into the driveway, the spot where she had run her new car into the junker.

"Your insurance premiums are going to go up like a Fourth of July rocket," Royce said, hearing her sigh.

"I know." Megan smothered another sigh. "But it was worth it to apprehend that terrible monster."

"Was it?" he demanded, bringing the car to a stop directly in front of the house.

"Yes, of course," she insisted, scrambling after him when he got out without a backward glance at her. "Royce, you must agree that it was worth it."

"Must I?" He turned from the door, which he had unlocked with her key, to give her a cool look. "Why must I?" He pushed the door open, stood aside, and motioned her to precede him.

Impatience and anxiety driving her, Megan hurried inside, then spun to face him as he followed and shut the door.

"Royce, please be reasonable about this," she said, prepared to plead with him if necessary. "I only wanted to help."

"You lied to me, Megan."

"But..." she began.

"Do all women lie to get their way?"

His voice held such anguish, it cut through her like a knife. Megan stared at him, and suddenly knew that he had been hurt, deeply hurt, by another woman who had lied to him.

"Royce, I..." she began again, but once more his voice sliced through hers.

"Dammit, Megan, I trusted you, believed in you." Striding to her, he grasped her by the shoulders. "You gave me your word, and then broke it the minute my back was turned."

"She hurt you very badly, didn't she?" Megan murmured, raising her hand to stroke his quivering face.

"Yes," he said bluntly. "But it was a shot to my ego and pride, not an emotionally lethal blow." His voice went low, soft and tender. "But it was nothing in comparison to the agony and trauma you've endured."

It was the opening she needed, and she grabbed for it. "But that's just it, Royce. It was because of the uncertainty and fear that I broke my word to you."

He frowned.

Megan rushed on. "After the way I fell apart last night, when that man called, I felt I had to do something to normalize my life, reclaim my sense of self. I just couldn't go on, being afraid of shadows, hiding behind you." She drew in a ragged breath. "Please, try to understand."

Royce's frown gave way to a rueful expression. "I do, now. And I'm sorry I yelled at you."

"I'm sorry, too." Megan hesitated, then asked the question she had to have answered. "Are you still missing her?"

"She doesn't matter anymore." His response came with satisfying swiftness. "She hasn't mattered for a long time. But you did."

Megan felt a searing twist of pain at his use of the past tense. Had her rash action destroyed her attraction for him? A rush of tears stung her eyes. "Did I?"

"Didn't last night prove that to you?"

"I thought," she said in a tear-choked whisper. "I hoped."

"I hoped, too." His fingers flexed, sinking sensuously into her soft flesh. "It's been nearly a year since I've been intimate with a woman." A wry smile slanted his lips. "Her defection left me feeling empty, sexually disinterested." His smile gentled. "Then I met you, and from that morning I came to interview you in the hospital, you filled me, brought back the wanting."

"Oh, Royce..."

"I know I have no right to dump my feelings on you, after what you've been through, but—" He drew a quick breath, then blurted out, "I'm afraid I'm falling in love with you, Megan." He gave a sharp shake of his head. "No, I know I'm in love with you."

The sensations that exploded inside Megan at his declaration were too glorious to be described. So she didn't even try. Instead, responding to them, she threw her arms around his neck and laughed in sheer joy and relief.

Royce reacted to the sound of her jubilation by releasing his hold on her arms to draw her close to him, very close. "Does this mean you don't mind?"

"Mind?" Megan's laughter peeled out again. "Oh, Sergeant, you big, beautiful man," she sang out when her laughter had subsided. "I'm very much afraid I'm in love with you, too. And the only thing I'd mind was if you didn't..."

His mouth claimed hers, drowning her voice, stirring her senses, sealing her fate. When, satisfying moments later, he raised his head, her eyes were shining with love for him as she finished what she'd begun to say.

"Want me, Wolfe."

* * * * *

COMING NEXT MONTH

Jilted!
They were left at the altar...
but not for long!

#889 THE ACCIDENTAL BRIDEGROOM—Ann Major

November's *Man of the Month* Rafe Steele never thought one night with
Cathy Calderon would make him a father. Now he had to find her before
she married someone else!

#890 TWO HEARTS, SLIGHTLY USED—Dixie Browning

Outer Banks

Frances Jones discovered the way to win sexy Brace Ridgeway was
through his stomach—until he got the flu and couldn't eat! But by then,
Brace only craved a sweet dessert called Frances....

#891 THE BRIDE SAYS NO—Cait London

Clementine Barlow gave rancher Evan Tanner a "Dear John" letter from
her sister, breaking their engagement. Even though the bride said no, will
this sister say yes?

#892 SORRY, THE BRIDE HAS ESCAPED—Raye Morgan

Ashley Carrington couldn't marry without love, so she ran off on her
wedding day. Was Kam Caine willing to risk falling in love to give this
former bride a chance?

#893 A GROOM FOR RED RIDING HOOD—Jennifer Greene

After being left at the altar, Mary Ellen Barnett knew she couldn't
trust anyone. Especially the wolf that lay underneath Steve Rawlings's
sexy exterior....

#894 BRIDAL BLUES—Cathie Linz

When Nick Grant came back home, Melissa Carlson enlisted his help to
win back her ex-fiancé. But once she succeeded, she realized it was Nick
she wanted to cure her bridal blues!

MILLION DOLLAR SWEEPSTAKES (III)

Dark secrets, dangerous desire...

Lovers
DARK AND
DANGEROUS

Three spine-tingling tales from the dark side of love.

This October, enter the world of shadowy romance as Silhouette presents the third in their annual tradition of thrilling love stories and chilling story lines. Written by three of Silhouette's top names:

**LINDSAY McKENNA
LEE KARR
RACHEL LEE**

Haunting a store near you this October.

Only from

Silhouette®

...where passion lives.

If you are looking for more titles by

JOAN HOHL

Don't miss this chance to order additional stories by
one of Silhouette's most popular authors:

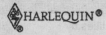

"HOORAY FOR HOLLYWOOD" SWEEPSTAKES

HERE'S HOW THE SWEEPSTAKES WORKS

OFFICIAL RULES — NO PURCHASE NECESSARY

To enter, complete an Official Entry Form or hand print on a 3" x 5" card the words "HOORAY FOR HOLLYWOOD", your name and address and mail your entry in the pre-addressed envelope (if provided) or to: "Hooray for Hollywood" Sweepstakes, P.O. Box 9076, Buffalo, NY 14269-9076 or "Hooray for Hollywood" Sweepstakes, P.O. Box 637, Fort Erie, Ontario L2A 5X3. Entries must be sent via First Class Mail and be received no later than 12/31/94. No liability is assumed for lost, late or misdirected mail.

Winners will be selected in random drawings to be conducted no later than January 31, 1995 from all eligible entries received.

Grand Prize: A 7-day/6-night trip for 2 to Los Angeles, CA including round trip air transportation from commercial airport nearest winner's residence, accommodations at the Regent Beverly Wilshire Hotel, free rental car, and $1,000 spending money. (Approximate prize value which will vary dependent upon winner's residence: $5,400.00 U.S.); 500 Second Prizes: A pair of "Hollywood Star" sunglasses (prize value: $9.95 U.S. each). Winner selection is under the supervision of D.L. Blair, Inc., an independent judging organization, whose decisions are final. Grand Prize travelers must sign and return a release of liability prior to traveling. Trip must be taken by 2/1/96 and is subject to airline schedules and accommodations availability.

Sweepstakes offer is open to residents of the U.S. (except Puerto Rico) and Canada who are 18 years of age or older, except employees and immediate family members of Harlequin Enterprises, Ltd., its affiliates, subsidiaries, and all agencies, entities or persons connected with the use, marketing or conduct of this sweepstakes. All federal, state, provincial, municipal and local laws apply. Offer void wherever prohibited by law. Taxes and/or duties are the sole responsibility of the winners. Any litigation within the province of Quebec respecting the conduct and awarding of prizes may be submitted to the Regie des loteries et courses du Quebec. All prizes will be awarded; winners will be notified by mail. No substitution of prizes are permitted. Odds of winning are dependent upon the number of eligible entries received.

Potential grand prize winner must sign and return an Affidavit of Eligibility within 30 days of notification. In the event of non-compliance within this time period, prize may be awarded to an alternate winner. Prize notification returned as undeliverable may result in the awarding of prize to an alternate winner. By acceptance of their prize, winners consent to use of their names, photographs, or likenesses for purpose of advertising, trade and promotion on behalf of Harlequin Enterprises, Ltd., without further compensation unless prohibited by law. A Canadian winner must correctly answer an arithmetical skill-testing question in order to be awarded the prize.

For a list of winners (available after 2/28/95), send a separate stamped, self-addressed envelope to: Hooray for Hollywood Sweepstakes 3252 Winners, P.O. Box 4200, Blair, NE 68009.

CBSRLS

OFFICIAL ENTRY COUPON

"Hooray for Hollywood"
SWEEPSTAKES!

Yes, I'd love to win the Grand Prize — a vacation in Hollywood —
or one of 500 pairs of "sunglasses of the stars"! Please enter me
in the sweepstakes!

This entry must be received by December 31, 1994.
Winners will be notified by January 31, 1995.

Name _____

Address _____ Apt. _____

City _____

State/Prov. _____ Zip/Postal Code _____

Daytime phone number _____
(area code)

Mail all entries to: Hooray for Hollywood Sweepstakes,
P.O. Box 9076, Buffalo, NY 14269-9076.
In Canada, mail to: Hooray for Hollywood Sweepstakes,
P.O. Box 637, Fort Erie, ON L2A 5X3.

KCH

OFFICIAL ENTRY COUPON

"Hooray for Hollywood"
SWEEPSTAKES!

Yes, I'd love to win the Grand Prize — a vacation in Hollywood —
or one of 500 pairs of "sunglasses of the stars"! Please enter me
in the sweepstakes!

This entry must be received by December 31, 1994.
Winners will be notified by January 31, 1995.

Name _____

Address _____ Apt. _____

City _____

State/Prov. _____ Zip/Postal Code _____

Daytime phone number _____
(area code)

Mail all entries to: Hooray for Hollywood Sweepstakes,
P.O. Box 9076, Buffalo, NY 14269-9076.
In Canada, mail to: Hooray for Hollywood Sweepstakes,
P.O. Box 637, Fort Erie, ON L2A 5X3.

KCH